CW01018855

This Old Shirt Of Mine

A 1950s urban idyll

By J. J. Rawlings

authorHOUSE™

1663 LIBERTY DRIVE, SUITE 200
BLOOMINGTON, INDIANA 47403
(800) 839-8640
WWW.AUTHORHOUSE.COM

First published by AuthorHouse 12/01/05

ISBN: 1-4208-8690-8 (sc)

Printed in the United States of America
Bloomington, Indiana

This book is printed on acid-free paper.

Contents

REFERENCES

1. 'The Street' by Harry Walters, published 1975 by Centreprise Publishing Project, 136 Kingsland High Street, London E9.

2. Cuttings (1963–1967) from the 'North London Press' and the 'Islington Gazette held at the Islington Local History Centre, Finsbury Library about the council's purchase of the flats following a long campaign by the Popham Street Tenants' Association.

3. Charles Booth's Survey of London (copyright held by the London School of Economics and Political Science): 1897 survey of the Popham Street area.

4. Article in the 'Islington Gazette', Friday January 6, 1967, about the proposed demolition of the Cottages.

5. 'Cathy Come Home', a film made for television in 1966, directed by Ken Loach. Cathy's family are made homeless and live temporarily in her mother–in–law's flat in the Cottages. The film depicts views of one of the 'Squares' during a five–minute run 15 minutes into the film.

THE COTTAGES

The Cottages ran along one side of Popham Street in the old market–garden village of Islington in the County of Middlesex. However, these cottages had been built in 1889 when London had long since swallowed up Islington and many other villages. As artisans' dwellings went these were not typical of Prince Albert's ideal cottages, the prototype of which still stands in Kennington Park. Nor were they influenced by the enlightened paternalistic company cottages erected by Titus Salt and the Cadbury chocolate company. These cottages were high rise, four storeys piled one upon the other. They were flats.

The Cottages were not owned by a charity like the Peabody or Samuel Lewis Trusts, or at least they were not when Jimmy Barton grew up there in the 1950s and 60s. They were run as a commercial enterprise and since the war had had a succession of owners with distinctive but unmemorable Eastern European names. When first built they were as good as any dwellings that Peabody or Guinness were providing, but years of neglect and war damage had turned the Cottages into grimy tenement slums.

There were four groups of flats designed to accommodate up to 1400 Cottagers at a density of 530 souls to the acre. In reality severe overcrowding could make the density far higher than this. Nevertheless the Cottages were in great demand from the beginning, and were indeed a big improvement on what the Cottagers had been used to. They were a step up. They provided lockable entrance gates for security. They had modern gas lighting, mains water, WCs and sinks, and a system of refuse collection. And they also provided some amenity in the form of a well kept 'keep off' garden in each courtyard. (For more information about the buildings see 'Architectural Notes'.)

Jimmy Barton's dad Charlie had been taken there as an infant in 1913 when the Cottages were still relatively new and well maintained. By 1922 his two bedroom flat at 57 Cornwall Cottages was home to nine members of his branch of the Barton family, which was not an unusual number to be living in one flat in those days. But such increases in the density of life put a great strain on the fabric of the buildings. After the Second World War the process of deterioration, fuelled by overcrowding and compounded by the Luftwaffe, was further exacerbated by a lack of investment as each new landlord maximised his profits by reducing his overheads. When Jimmy Barton was born in the back bedroom of No. 83 Cornwall Cottages in 1947 (see illustration 3), the blocks of flats were well on their way to becoming warrens of slums, notorious for violence, crime, poverty and squalor. But Jimmy Barton only began to think of the scene of his happy childhood in this way some decades later, after the Cottages had been demolished and when his horizons had widened. Perhaps he had been lucky. The seamier side of Cottage life had never seemed to spoil his pleasure in being a street kid. His family life was full of laughter, and his parents' love and instinctive honesty had insulated him from the worst temptations of Street life. Of course he was not the only Cottage kid with these advantages and in some respects the notoriety of the Cottages was undeserved. Jimmy liked where he lived but then he did not know any better.

The Cottages were not the only blocks of flats in the 'Street' as the road that served them was commonly called. On the other side of the cobbled road, at the top end, was the even less salubrious Quinn Buildings, and at the bottom was a new, small block of council flats called Finnemore House. Also, behind the Cottages in Pickering Street were more walk–up tenements. Apart from the council flats all of these buildings were developed at the same time and all had reached their nadir by the 1950s. Although the density of occupation on and near the Street was suffocating, the post–war generation of Cottage kids had the benefit of the 'brown lungs' which the Luftwaffe had created. The adjacent 'bomb ruins' had been cleared of rubble but were not yet completely built over with new council flats. Islington Council seemed to have run out of redevelopment steam after the Tory success in the 1951 General Election, or at least it appeared to have done in this part of south Islington. The ruins were a great resource, and a release for the school–milk–fuelled energy of Cottage youth.

The four groups of tenements had been given evocative names. The group at the top of the Street was called Edinburgh Cottages, then came Cornwall Cottages where Jimmy Barton lived, followed by Queens Cottages, and Albany Cottages at the bottom. It was not the buildings themselves which defined the four groups of flats so much as the courtyards, each of which was known as the 'Square'(See illustration 8), and no two were exactly alike nor were any of them truly square. Separating the side blocks of each of the Squares were narrow canyons, only 25ft or so wide. These dank and gloomy spaces only allowed a little light and air to reach the bedroom windows facing each other across the void. They were ironically known as 'Aireys'(See illustration 8). On one long side of each Airey was a four–foot change of level. This was protected by a chain–link fence only eight feet away from the ground floor bedroom windows, which looked straight on to a slimy retaining wall and the fence above it.

It was possible to walk from one Square to the next at ground level by way of the Aireys, but not by way of the open access balconies, and it was this disconnection that reinforced the power of the Squares to define each group of tenements and to some extent each community of Cottagers as well. Each Square was strangely unique and instantly recognisable, and the Cottagers, especially the kids, were loyal to their Square and just a little territorial.

The long main block facing the Street, grew straight out of the pavement and was pierced by four arched, two storey high openings leading into each of the Squares. These openings provided the only official access to the tenements. Unofficially, of course, tenants or burglars could climb in the ground floor bedroom windows from the Street. The archways were originally provided with iron gates that could be secured at night and each entrance space had from the beginning been known as the 'Gate'. This name had stuck right down to Jimmy's generation and beyond, even though the ironwork had been removed years before and melted down to aid the war effort.

The Aireys, the balconies, the open staircases, the Gates and the Squares, with their central gardens now concreted over after the air raid shelters were removed, together with the bomb ruins formed one huge playground for Jimmy and his friends. Its layout was forever incised in their memory (See illustration 1.)

Jimmy Barton's flat was situated on the top balcony of Cornwall Cottages facing south across the Square towards the Gate (See illustrations 1 and 2). It was sunnier and airier than most of the flats and also it had no heavy–footed neighbours overhead. The bedroom windows at the back looked straight on to the windows of the tenements in Pickering Street. In the chasm below, spiked railings separated the Pickering pavement from the narrow sunken area in front of the ground floor Cornwall bedrooms. Upon these railings an unfortunate Cottager had once been impaled by her husband, who threw her out of a window.

In the summertime Charlie Barton would sit outside his front door or lean on the railings smoking and watching the comings and goings of people in the Square and on the open staircases and balconies. But in winter the balconies and stairs gave no protection to homecoming cottagers what with rain pouring through the open risers and with the Square being criss–crossed with lethal slides made in the snow by winter booted Cottage kids. However old Mrs. Smith was quite content when it rained because she could drag out her huge potted aspidistras for a good watering on the top landing of the staircase outside her front door.

On fine days Jimmy's mum would often leave baby James parked on the balcony in his pushchair and clutching his beloved teddy bear. In the post–war austerity toys were hard to come by and Charlie Barton had done wonders finding his son a teddy bear at all in that awful winter of 1947. But Jack, the Brison's terrier from the other side of the Square, had not an ounce of sentiment in him. He would sneak up on Jimmy and snatch his teddy bear away. Jimmy would bawl and his mother would dash out of the flat to see what all the commotion was about and chase Jack around the balcony, trying to corner the thief before he savaged the teddy beyond repair. By the end of his babyhood Jimmy's teddy had no arms or legs and only one ear although Mrs Barton did her best to re–stuff it's torso. This was Jimmy's first encounter with the tribulations of Cottage life. Jimmy had been too young to recall for himself the depredations of Jack but the teddy bear survived to recount the story many years later.

As soon as he could walk Jimmy was allowed to play on the balcony when his mum or dad were there. He would sit with his legs dangling between the railings over the edge of the balcony and watch the older kids playing in the Square below. He was desperate to get down there with them, and it was not long before he too was 'raking' in the dirt.

In the early 1950s the ground floor flats of Cornwall Cottages were being modernised, a process which quickly ran out of money. However for as long as it lasted the kids had a wonderful time playing in the builders' sand and climbing up the sacks of cement. It was while the building work was going on that Jimmy fell through the balcony. Fortunately he only fell from the first floor and landed, just a bit awkwardly, on some sand. A baluster was missing from the railings and Jimmy, being shorter than the top rail, just fell through. His teenage sister Sally had seen him fall, looking in disbelief as he landed like 'a sack of potatoes', she said. Doctor Karson found no serious injuries and Jimmy was soon passed raking fit again. But the incident caused a bit of a fuss at the time. Jimmy's mum ticked off the agent in the rent office, and also the caretaker when she eventually found him, and afterwards, for a while at least, such safety hazards were promptly dealt with and the builders' materials kept out of harms way. All of the balconies had loose and missing balusters but Jimmy had happened to fall through the only gap that had not been wired up. There were still wired up gaps in the railings almost two decades later when the Cottages were knocked down. As far as he knew Jimmy was the only kid to fall off a balcony although plenty had jumped, usually on to old mattresses.

Jimmy spent his last pre–school days under the watchful eyes of his mother looking down from the balcony above. He raked in the Square with his new found friend Terry, and discovered the differences between girls and boys with the little girl who lived next to Terry and who was known at the time as 'Did–a–wee', for obvious reasons. They spent many idyllic hours delving into drain gratings, digging dirt out of manhole handles and from the cracks in the concrete paving, scratching doodles with stones and bits of chalk, collecting piles of dirt and learning how to throw and catch and kick a ball. Then one dreadful day Mrs. Barton dragged Jimmy away from the pile of lolly sticks he had collected, wiped him over with a damp hankie, and marched him protesting out of the Square and down to Charlie Mutton's Infants for his first afternoon at school. Jimmy thought that his visit to the school was just a temporary phenomenon. But from then on his mother would take him to school every day and bring him home at lunchtimes for tinned vegetable soup and 'Listen With Mother' on the radio. Then he was taken back again for the afternoon summer nap on the 'Z beds' which were set up in the bottom playground for the very youngest children (the older and more boisterous infants were suitably contained behind the high chain link fencing of the rooftop playground). But all Jimmy wanted to do was to play with Terry in the Square. However Terry was also going to school, it was a different one in Canonbury. Jimmy only escaped once when he woke naturally from his playground slumber and absent–mindedly walked out of the playground without anybody noticing. Horrified, Mrs. Barton took him straight back to school where the teachers were noticeably relieved at his return. There was probably no connection, but during the three years he spent at the Infants after that not once did he get to play the tambourine or the triangle. They only ever gave him a pair of sticks to bang together.

By the time Jimmy had moved from the Infants to Charlie Mutton Juniors across the alley, which ran up the side of the 'Barley Mow' pub and smelled deliciously of horses, he had become a fully–fledged Street raker. He was now allowed to play on the bomb ruins and in the Street as well as in the Square, providing he did not wander off.

Apart from grazes and cuts his early years as a raker only cost him a couple of whitlows, chapped legs and pains in his shins, which his mother said was rheumatism. However his mum did have to lay him out face down on newspaper on the kitchen table once or twice to be de–wormed.

His mum stopped taking him to school a year or so later and let him go down to Charlie Mutton's on his own. The boys' playground opened on to Pickering Street at the bottom and Mrs. Barton would hang out of her bedroom window and watch out for Jimmy as he crowded into the school with the other kids. Jimmy had instructions to wave at the distant object protruding from the long wall of the Cottages half way up the street, and he would only go into the playground when this object waved back. Some of the tougher boys from the Street thought that Jimmy was a bit of a sissy for doing this, and he was relieved when his mum finally trusted his good sense enough to get herself a part time job. With his mother's blessing and the admonition of 'don't get into mischief' he had finally graduated into fully unencumbered street life.

GAMES

Running games were popular all year round with the kids from Cornwall Cottages, especially the game known as 'King–he'. The person who was 'On' would be chosen by the ancient hand shaking contest called 'chewing up' in which an open hand (paper) covers a fist (stone), which blunts a pair of open fingers (scissors), which cuts an open hand, or something like that. The chosen one would then proceed to take careful aim with a frayed tennis ball and throw it at any of the other players who had by then quickly dispersed around the Square. It was a strict rule that no one was allowed to run while holding the ball. With half a dozen moving targets to choose from, the best strategy for the lone ball thrower was to roll it into a good position first, run up to it and then throw it straight and hard,into a bunch of yelling fugitives.

Stone throwing practice on the bomb ruins had made the Cottage kids expert shots and very soon someone would be hit with the ball, and this allowed the game to move up a gear. Now two people would be 'On' and both could aim the ball at the remaining players, and they could pass the ball to each other. Life for those remaining became more precarious as the game proceeded. Soon there would be three and then four throwers and subsequently fewer and fewer targets for whom there was no longer safety in numbers. And so tactics were changed. The targets would now keep well clear of each other to avoid being hit by default, and the ball throwers did more passing and less running. Finally only one quarry would be left, the one who had been most skilled at twisting and turning, feinting his moves and anticipating the moves of the throwers, and the one who had the most luck. He, for usually only boys played 'King–he', would be brought to ground exhausted, and the game would start all over again.

'King–he' was great fun, and noisy, but it had its drawbacks. Sometimes the ball would split someone's lip or redden his ear, but worse than that, it might hit a door or a window and bring out an irate Cottager. If a door was opened some of the children would slip into the Aireys out of sight, but others would brave the onslaught.

*

"Clear off and take that bloody ball with you!" Said Mr. Donohue.

He was standing on the threshold of his ground floor flat in his slippers.

"You've been banging that ball on my wall all bleedin' day."

"This is our first game Mr. Donohue." Terry had a strong sense of injustice.

"And you was out 'ere yesterday an' all, an' nearly broke the winder."

"That wasn't us!"

Mr. Donohue had better things to do than to remonstrate with a load of kids, especially now that he had acquired a television set.

"I'll have none of your cheek. Any more out o' you an' I'll be up to see your Nan. Go orn, an' clear off. Half of you don't live round 'ere anyway. Why don't you play outside your own front doors?"

So the game was suspended to allow Mr. Donohue to return to Michael Miles and 'Take Your Pick', and the players sloped off to the Gate for a post mortem discussion.

*

On the whole the ground floor Cottagers were a tolerant lot. Many had young children of their own who played in the Square, and it was mostly childless couples or those with grown up children like Mr Donohue and Mr. Sears who had it in for the kids in the Square. Mr. Sears once gave Terry a clout for answering back. Terry's mum found out and she knocked up Mr. Sears to sort him out. Having received a load of abuse she then fetched her husband, Terry's stepfather, and the Square was treated to a stand up fight. The kids loved it. The neighbours lined the balconies and gathered in muttering groups in the Square. The fight, preceded by an exchange of compliments, sapped the strength of the two grown ups whose fighting days were long passed. Mrs. Sears and Terry's mum joined in to defend their respective champions. It ended as it began with a stand off exchange of expletives. Terry's stepfather never found the jumper he had removed before rolling up his sleeves and Mr. Sears thought twice before sorting out the kids playing in the Square again.

There were other games similar to 'King–he' such as 'Knocking–down Sticks', 'Queen–he' and the very noisy 'Tin–Tan Tommy' which involved the banging of a tin can on the grating of one of the drain holes in the Square.

'Knocking–down Sticks' was almost as popular as 'King–he'. Four short sticks of firewood were placed against a wall in cricket wicket fashion. The boys divided into two teams. The first team had three throws at the sticks with a tennis ball. As soon as one or more of the sticks had been knocked over, the members of the team would run off in all directions across the Square and the Gate. The second team meanwhile would scramble for the ball and, as in 'King–he', proceed to pick off the members of the first team one by one. Once they were hit with the ball they were out of the game. In the general melee brave and wily members of the first team would attempt to rebuild the wicket, making sitting targets of themselves at the same time. The winning team had either rebuilt the sticks into some semblance of a wicket, or had caught with the ball all of the members of the opposing team before they could do so.

The extra thrill of trying to put up the fallen wicket before being struck from behind with a well aimed tennis ball, made the game more exciting and even noisier than 'King–he'. The shouts of encouragement and of warning would reverberate around the walls and balconies of the flats. 'Knocking–down Sticks' was not appreciated by the Cottagers not only because of the noise but also because it was centred on the Gate through which every Cottager had to pass at some time. The children chose the Gate because it had two blank walls without windows or doors against which the ball could be thrown without damaging anything.

They usually leaned the sticks against the wall belonging to the flat occupied by the Doolan family, some of whose younger members were ardent knockers–down of sticks, and under the sign that said 'No Hawkers, No Canvassers, No Ball Games'. Mrs. Doolan was a small jovial Irish woman up to her ears in kids, and the ball banging on her wall made little difference to the hubbub inside her flat. However, Mr. Doolan, home from work heavy footed and by way of the Half Moon, would ear tweak his eldest sons indoors and disperse the rest of the players with a black glare and a back hander swung in their general direction.

The dark evenings of winter would put a premature stop to ball games, but the darkness made it possible to play

'Run–outs'. This was a game that took in not only the Square and the Gate but also the Squares and the Gates and Aireys of all the neighbouring Cottages, and even the adjacent streets. It was a game of stealth causing little disturbance, which in the foreign territory of somebody else's Square was a distinct advantage. The game was simple. One team would 'run–out' and disappear into the shadows of the buildings to be hunted out by the other team after a count of two hundred, which was always chanted aloud in fives. After lying low for a while the members of the hunted team would cautiously make their way back to where the game had started while trying not to be spotted.

*

"75, 80, 85, 90, 95, a hundred.... Coming!" Terry finished the count and the team of hunters split up, Jimmy and Alan searched the Squares and Aireys and Terry and Barry patrolled the Street, the ruins and the Gates. They had agreed to meet up again at the bottom of the Street if no one had been flushed out in the meantime.

It was a cold night and Alan only had his school jersey on, and he was still in short trousers. But he was wiry and strong for his age. Jimmy was more sensibly dressed. His mother had put him into long trousers at an early age because he was tall and plump, and he always wore a jacket, indoors as well as outdoors, in summer and of course in winter when the cuff of the left sleeve gained a shiny patina from runny nose wiping. He used to hate wearing short trousers in winter because he always got 'chapped' legs especially on the inside of his thighs. Alan and Jimmy loped off across the Cornwall Square and into the corner passage that led to the Airey from where steps led down to the Queens Square. The narrow Airey between the two parallel blocks of Cottages was set aside for drying washing but was hardly ever used as the sun barely reached it (See illustration 8).

The Airey was very still. The new frost on the asphalt reflected the faint light coming from the solitary lamppost. The boys peered down the 100ft length of the Airey and then up to the access balconies that served those flats unfortunate enough to have their front doors overlooking it. They could see and hear no one. Alan whispered that he would look down the dark end of the Airey and silently ran off, carefully side–stepping the slippery patches of muddy residue that formed at the edges of the Airey's permanent winter puddles. At the end of the Airey two more passages connected the Squares but these were obstructed by railings. Few people ever had cause to come here, but it was a favourite haunt of courting cats. Alan climbed the railings and jumped down into the lower level on the Queens' side. He stood outside the door of the empty flat used in the past for storing building materials, but now it was deserted and the door was off its hinges. Alan's bravery did not extend to delving in the dark passage leading into the flat to look for 'run–out' fugitives. So he continued into the corner of Queens' Square, glad to leave the claustrophobic Airey behind. He met Jimmy who ran up from the adjacent corner having entered the Square from the other end of the Airey by way of the steps provided for the purpose. Queens Cottages were deserted except for a few kids sitting on the stairs in the Gate.

So they continued their search through the almost identical passages and Airey that separated Queens from Albany Cottages. The L shaped Square of Albany was virtually a foreign land to the Cornwall boys. They knew that the runaways they were hunting would feel uncomfortable here too, so they headed out through the Albany Gate and into the Street.

Terry and Barry were sitting on the tubular rail above the low boundary wall of the small council housing estate on the other side of the Street.

"Seen anyone?" Barry shouted as Jimmy and Alan appeared in the Albany Gate.

"Nah," they said in unison.

"I bet they've gone right round to Pickering Street," suggested Jimmy as he reached the wall.

"I thought that was against the rules," said Barry.

Jimmy climbed on to the concrete coping of the brick pier at the end of the wall and began a tightrope walk along the tubular rail.

"Don't move then!" he yelled as he reached the seated Terry, and losing his balance he chose to jump into the plant bed on the opposite side of the wall.

Terry laughed.

"Well I'm going back. It's bloody freezing," declared Alan.

"Me an' all," said Barry.

"You're not going in then, are you?" Terry asked.

"Might."

"But we ain't 'ad our run–out yet," Terry complained as he watched the two boys striding off up the Street, "Come on, don't be spoilsports," he shouted after them.

Jimmy climbed back over the wall. He and Terry decided to walk round to Pickering Street anyway. Firstly they rounded Albany into Popham Road, known to the boys as 'going down the bottom', and then they headed up Pickering Street. They passed the boys' playground of Charlie Mutton Juniors and then crossed to the other side of the street to avoid walking past the staircase entrances of its run down tenements. The windows of these flats looked straight across the street into the bedrooms of the Cottages. Four older boys emerged out of the last entrance. Jimmy and Terry came level and the boys began to follow them. One of them called out 'Who you screwing?' This was the accepted opening gambit to start a fight. Terry was always willing to stick up for himself but Jimmy was in a panic.

Terry also felt outnumbered and they independently decided on a quick departure. They ran up the street towards Essex Road with the others not far behind. The pursuers in 'Run–outs' became the pursued and they kept on running, along Essex Road to the Half Moon pub and then down the Street until they got to Terry's mum's flat on the ground floor of Cornwall Cottages.

"What's the matter with you two?" asked his mother.

"Nuffin', just a game," panted Terry.

"Those mates of yours were looking for you," she said.

"Who, Mike and Steve?"

"Yes. I think that's who it was. They said they weren't waiting any longer for you to find them and they were going home, they looked frozen."

If it went on for too long 'Run–outs' could get boring.

*

The Gate was irresistible as a playground because it was sheltered from the rain and it connected the Square with the Street. It also had two flights of stairs with a connecting balcony at first floor level that made it ideal for chase games. All the kids used to slide down the banisters, but the stairs were also jumped by older foolhardy boys clearing all sixteen steps to soft land on old mattresses. The Gate's main drawback for Cottage youth was it's function as the major crossroads of the Cottages where passing adults would stop for a chat or to read a sad note of thanks for neighbourly condolences taped to the wall by a bereaved Cottager. However play could proceed largely uninterrupted if the kids avoided the Cottage rush hours. Apart from 'Queen–he', 'Knocking–down Sticks' and a spitting game called 'Watering Can', the Gate was also suitable for the more intimate pursuits of 'Jimmy Nacker' and 'Under the Coats'.

'Jimmy Nacker' was a traditional game but it was losing its popularity. It was a rough game that tested the strength and resolve of the players. This may explain the use of the colloquial word 'Nacker'. The older children initiated each new generation into the 'Jimmy Nacker' tradition – a sort of trial by ordeal. The players would form themselves into a circular chain. Each boy would be bent over in Rugby scrum fashion with his head tucked well down and his shoulders pressed against the buttocks in front, and with his hands gripping the trouser waist band. The circle would revolve at increasing speed until it broke. The break would occur at the weakest link, which was usually one of the younger players, and he would lead the chain to the side wall of the Gate. More often than not it would be the Doolan side.

The boys would all bend over again and the boy at the front would lean hard against the wall with his head resting on his forearms. The chain of people behind him would now be attached umbilically to the wall as it were, and the player at the free end would detach himself and after a suitable run up would leapfrog over the boy who now formed the end of the chain. Having landed heavily on somebody's neck or back he would move up to the head of the chain by placing his hands on the backs of those beneath and would swing himself along from person to person. He would immediately be followed by the next boy on the end, and so it went on until as many leap–froggers as possible were sitting astride what was left of the original chain. Then the chanting would begin and the boys on top would leap up and down like demented horse riders.

"Jimmy Jimmy Nacker, one two three, one two three, one two three. Jimmy Jimmy Nacker, one two three," the chorus would echo around the Gate accompanied by grunts, squeals and protests. The frogs at the bottom would swing violently from side to side as backs, necks and arms took a pounding from above, and legs would be braced to take the strain. The object of all this effort was to cause the edifice to collapse in as few choruses of the 'Jimmy Nacker' chant as possible. After a bruising game of 'Jimmy Nacker' it was difficult to get enough people interested in another, that is until the next generation was up for initiation.

Far less exhausting was the game known as 'Under the Coats'. This was played beneath the light of the big electric lamp in the Gate on dark winter evenings when coats were available. Two teams would make a pile of their coats, and then one team would wander off, out of sight and ear–shot, into the Square. The other team would proceed to cover up one or more of its members with the coats. Great care would be taken to conceal every recognisable part of those willing to sit or crouch or lie on the bare cold concrete paving. When every chink in the pile had been plugged, the remaining members of the team would hide, usually behind the parked cars in the Street just outside the Gate, and one of them would call out a heavily disguised "Ready!"

The other team would hurry back into the Gate and try to guess who had been buried. But before a declaration was made, they would crack jokes, abuse reputations and scrutinise the whole rag–bag in great detail. Mounds and protuberances would be compared unfavourably with the anatomies of the members of the other team. In this way it was hoped to extract a movement or a recognisable grunt or titter from those suffocating inside the heap of coats. As soon as the declaration was made the coats would erupt and people would appear from behind cars and walls and an uproarious inquest would follow. Unfortunately this game was usually short lived because of the pressing need for the coats to be reassigned to their proper function.

The Gate was famous for being the venue of the great annual marbles tournaments which would go on for days during the summer. The small glass balls were prized possessions, especially the newest types known as 'Cat's

Eyes', which were clear glass with brightly coloured streaks in the centre. It seemed that nobody ever bought marbles in shops, yet everybody appeared to have them. They were just sort of acquired, and every summer thousands of them changed hands. The main playing area was situated under the central stair landing where the Gate joined the Square and where there was a large rectangular cast iron manhole cover. This had a regular pattern of raised square studs on its surface, and near each end it had a sunken handgrip. It was on this ready–made bagatelle board that marble fortunes were won and lost.

The studs on the manhole cover ran in parallel lines so that there were unobstructed grooves, just wide enough to give the marbles a clear run between the rows of studs in both a north/south and an east/west direction. The two sunken handgrips were each served by four pairs of these grooves coming from the four points of the compass. The object of the game was to win back as many marbles as possible by getting them into the sunken hand grips and the easiest way to do this was to shoot the marbles along the grooves leading directly into them.

Before a tournament could begin, it was necessary for the cover to be cleared of dirt and small stones, and for the accumulation of debris to be dug out of the handgrips using lolly sticks. A crease line would then be chalked on the ground about six feet from the manhole cover and from behind this crease each player in turn would shoot marbles on to the cover. The order of play would be decided beforehand according to who could get their marble nearest to the hand grip in one throw. Also the number of players and the number of marbles to be played in each game would be agreed.

When all the formalities had been settled the first game could commence. If it were a two hander, ten–up game, the first player would roll his ten marbles one at a time over the concrete paving and on to the manhole cover. He would aim each one at the two grooves leading directly into the handgrip, and would retrieve all those that ended up there. The second player would then shy his ten marbles on to the manhole cover and similarly would recover any marbles that rolled into or were cannoned into the handgrip.

However most of the marbles would hit the first row of studs and bounce away in haphazard fashion over the manhole cover and the paving around it, and the first player would now have the opportunity of pocketing these errant marbles. With the use of a crooked index finger placed behind a likely marble he would flick it towards the handgrip. If the marble was in one of the grooves leading into the handgrip, a simple putt was all that was needed to sink it. However, shots from other parts of the manhole cover were more difficult, but a technique had been perfected of flicking a marble lying next to a stud in such a way that it lifted and flew off towards the hand grip like a tiddlywink. There was something deeply satisfying in the clack of the marbles in the handgrip as another joined them. After an unsuccessful shot by a player, the second player would take his turn, as in a game of snooker. The game finished when the last marble was pocketed. The player with more marbles than he started with would be well satisfied and the loser would seek a return match to recover his losses.

*

Raymond Bishop and John Winston, two of the older Cornwall boys, were the marbles kings of the Square. It was rumoured that they had won thousands of marbles each in the tournaments over the years. They were both happy to play the younger and less skilful boys but had mostly avoided playing each other. Inevitably there was great speculation in the Square about who was the best player. It came to the point where people became dissatisfied with playing small–time marbles among themselves. The pressure for a show down between the marbles kings became irresistible.

Raymond was a year older than John. He seldom played with the other children in the Square unless the game involved gambling or winning prized possessions like picture cards and marbles. He would fleece the younger boys at 'Penny–up–the–Wall' and 'Pontoon' but would otherwise spend little of his time in the Square. He was strong and well built and liked to get his own way and hardly any of the children were brave enough to refuse him a game. Indeed they were pleased that he spent so little time in the Square. Yet their ambivalence towards Raymond, if anything, made the prospect of a decisive marbles match even more exhilarating.

John was altogether a different kind of boy. Although relatively tall and physically mature for his age he was plump and not at all athletic. Like Raymond he no longer joined in the games played in the Square unless they involved the opportunity for gain. But unlike Raymond he was not intimidating and did not hang around with the local toughs. He was secretive and would talk to the other boys in conspiratorial whispers. The boys of Cornwall Cottages admired him for his prowess at marbles and envied his ability to hang on to money for longer than five minutes.

It was Jimmy Barton who eventually acted as go–between. John did not have any close friends among the boys in the Square but he knew Jimmy quite well because their mothers were long time acquaintances. Jimmy would be sent down to Winnie, as John's mother was known, with some mending or alterations his mother had done or to pick up a bit of shopping Winnie had done in return. It was on one of these errands that Jimmy brought up the subject of marbles with John. Eventually Jimmy got John to agree to challenge Raymond for the title of 'champeen marble king' providing

Jimmy did the negotiating and there were sufficient marbles at stake to make it worth while.

Raymond Bishop was in the Gate winning a few marbles from Alan when Jimmy got around to asking him if he wanted a game with John Winston. Although Jimmy was wary of Raymond he no longer held him in awe – not since the day he had bragged about the toy binoculars his sister had given him for his birthday. Jimmy had insisted that they were real. Raymond had disagreed and Jimmy, who honestly believed that they were authentic binoculars, was finally goaded into threatening to thump the next boy who contradicted him. Raymond obliged and Jimmy hit him. Of course it was Jimmy who was thumped and left bawling on the ground more out of frustration than anything else. Raymond must have felt a little mean about this incident because he was slightly less dismissive with Jimmy than he was with some of the other boys.

Jimmy appealed to Raymond's vanity as the best player down the Street and then introduced John's upstart challenge. Although Raymond had found that his interest in winning marbles from the boys in the Square had been waning lately in favour of more adult interests such as girls, smoking and punch ups in the wider world, this was a challenge he could not let pass. He downed the last of Alan's marbles and drew the strings on his marbles bag and stuffed it in his pocket. As he strolled away he dismissively ordered Jimmy to bring John and his marbles into the Gate on the following evening.

After school the next day a larger than usual gang of boys and a few curious girls had gathered in the Gate. They had already been the cause of admonitory remarks from Cottagers coming home from work, generally cursing kids who were always blocking up the stairs. They were all waiting for Raymond to turn up. John had been nervously hanging around in the Gate since he had got home. Raymond and John both went to Queen's Head Street School, the local Secondary Modern, but they were in different years, and after school Raymond had not come straight home but had been having a smoke with his friends and had forgotten about the game.

"Here's Ray coming down the Street," shouted Barry who had appointed himself as lookout, "He's with his brother."

A few boys went to see for themselves just as Raymond and his older brother Peter turned into the Gate.

"Hey Ray, what about the big marbles match?" Terry asked as Raymond and his brother started to climb the stairs in the Gate. Their flat was on the first floor balcony above the Doolan residence. They both stopped and looked over the staircase hand rail. Raymond carelessly aimed a gob of spit at one of the boys below. It missed.

"Oh yeah, Johnny Winston wants to lose his marbles," said Raymond.

"What's all this then?" jibed his older brother, "You ain't still playing bleedin' marbles, you big kid?"

Peter climbed the remaining stairs laughing as he went and turned along the balcony to his flat. Raymond did not like to be laughed at but although bigger than his brother he was no match for him. He would have preferred to forget the marbles match altogether but he did not want to lose face with the kids in the Square as well as with his brother. He followed Peter up the stairs but came back a few minutes later carrying a patched home made plimsoll bag stuffed with beautiful 'Cat's Eyes'.

"OK Johnny boy, What's it to be?" said Raymond as the crowd of children parted to make way. Two little kids scrambled up their marbles from the manhole cover that was to be the field of play for the great marbles contest, and merged into the crowd.

"How about thirty–up to begin with?" suggested John who was clutching a heavy biscuit tin containing marbles under his arm. The two protagonists were standing in front of the manhole cover between the two parallel flights of stairs, and the silent spectators were gathered expectantly around the other three sides of the cover.

"Look," said Raymond, "I ain't got all night to piss about with you lot," he paused, "One game, two hundred–up or nothing."

A gasp of amazement went up from the crowd. John was unperturbed.

"OK," he said thoughtfully, "But how're we gonna do it?"

"I reckon we should take turns with ten–up until they're all played and we keep any that go in either of the handles – alright?" Raymond expected no objection.

"Alright by me," said John.

The game began. Nobody could remember anybody ever playing two hundred–up; thirty or forty, but two hundred never. John's marble was nearest the hole so he began the game. He sent up his first ten marbles. He had got his eye in by the third and he placed the next three into the grooves between the studs on the cover leading directly into the nearest recessed handle. He also cannoned another into the hole and so he retrieved four of his ten marbles.

Before Raymond took his turn he pointed at Jimmy and ordered, "You can keep count Jimbo."

"Sure Ray," said Jimmy who was often called upon to be the arbiter of fair play in the games played by the kids in the Square.

Raymond only managed to recover two of his marbles before Jimmy called out "Twenty–up" and John's second set of ten were heading over the concrete paving towards the iron cover. By the time one hundred marbles had been played the cover was smothered in 'Cat's Eyes' and surrounded by stray marbles that had ricocheted off the metal studs or had cannoned off other marbles. It was no longer possible to get a clear shot at the holes from the crease.

"Sixty–up," called Jimmy.

"Hold it," said Raymond before sending up his sixth set of marbles, "We've got to get some of these marbles out of the way." He expected no contradiction.

"If I get a marble down on this go I'll start potting the ones on the cover."

All eyes turned to Jimmy. Although Jimmy thought that the privilege of going first should be earned through 'chewing up', spinning a coin or something, he did not object to the proposal. Nobody expected anything else from Jimmy because Raymond was not to be crossed, and so Jimmy kept his reputation as honest broker even after this obvious lapse. John was unconcerned, as he had already retrieved twenty marbles whereas Raymond had only salvaged twelve and John was confident that he could outplay Raymond any day on the manhole cover.

Having cannoned a marble in, Raymond now began to push the nearest marbles one at a time into the handles. He had downed ten marbles before he fell foul of a difficult shot and it was John's turn. The area around the holes were clearer now and John accurately potted five of the ten marbles he sent up and then he proceeded to clear away a further six of those closest to the holes. There were still nearly eighty marbles strewn around the manhole cover when he missed his seventh putt. Raymond and everyone else looking on could see that John was coming out on top. Raymond counted out another ten marbles. Jimmy called out, "Seventy–up". Raymond lowered his hand level with the ground and loosed all ten in one go towards the manhole cover. One marble went in.

"What ya doing Ray? Asked Jimmy as Raymond counted out another ten marbles and the spectators looked on aghast.

"It's taking too long," Raymond replied, and he sent another ten up, and then another.

When Jimmy called out, "One hundred", Raymond stopped the onslaught and went over to the manhole cover to empty the recessed handles of the half dozen marbles that had found their way there. It was difficult to find places to stand near the cover but Raymond kicked a few marbles out of the way so that he could get at the potted marbles and the many likely shots that surrounded the holes. He emptied the handles, took careful aim and flicked a marble into the nearest hole, but it shot up it's sloping side and landed back on the manhole cover.

Raymond swore. John once more took up his position and counted the marbles out of his tin.

"You've got to do forty–up like me," Raymond demanded.

John obliged and sent them up in four waves. At the end of his go he had recovered twenty. With only half the marbles played the cover and the surrounding paving was already crowded with shining pieces of glass. The children had now formed a wider circle around the growing area of play and the Gate was effectively blocked. Raymond now resumed his position behind the line.

"Lend us the lid of your tin?" he said to John, "Come on, I won't nick it," he added as he saw a worried look come over John's face.

In amazement the crowd watched as Raymond counted fifty marbles from his bag into the upturned lid. He picked the lid up with two hands and tossed the marbles in the direction of the manhole cover and a cheer went up from the crowd. Marbles were rebounding everywhere. Sections of the crowd opened up as marbles came careering towards them.

A few strays ended up lost forever in nearby drain holes that had the gratings missing. Raymond now found it difficult to get near the handles to empty them without knocking lots of marbles out of court, but he was not bothered.

John sent the next fifty marbles up and afterwards succeeded in recovering a great many of those that were crowded around the holes. Raymond followed with a further fifty and Jimmy ceremoniously called out "Two hundred–up". The Gate was now awash with marbles.

Mr. Doolan was not the first Cottager to attempt a crossing of the Gate. Others had preceded him. Some took a fleeting interest in the gathering of children and moved on when they realised that it was only a game of marbles, and some complained about children blocking the Gate. But unfortunately Mr. Doolan trod on a wayward marble as he was easing his way through the crowd, and he fell heavily against the wall. His face darkened and he mumbled an awful Gaelic curse as he recovered his feet. Some of the children turned around to find out what the disturbance was and seeing that it was only Mr. Doolan home from work, they carried on watching the game. They had no intention of letting adult sensibilities spoil their enjoyment of the biggest marbles game they had ever seen.

Mr. Doolan reached out towards two boys who were standing behind one of the steel stanchions that held up the balcony above the manhole cover.

"Yous two," he growled, "In!"

He loomed over the two eldest Doolan boys with one arm raised and the other pointing towards the Doolan residence. They shot off in the direction indicated just as the pointing hand was lifted into a more threatening gesture. Mr. Doolan slowly followed and all three disappeared into the passage of number twenty Cornwall Cottages. The boys later returned to the game after Mrs. Doolan had calmed down their father and presented him with his dinner.

Meanwhile Raymond and John continued to take turns at potting the marbles and great shouts went up whenever a difficult shot found its mark. After an unusually successful break by John, Raymond conceded defeat.

"OK Johnny boy, you can have the rest," he said. Those in the crowd who had ever had dealings with Raymond stood open mouthed at this uncharacteristic gesture. Raymond pushed his way out of the circle of bemused spectators. He walked back into the Gate and ran two at a time up the stairs to the first floor balcony. Outside his flat he paused and moved towards the railings calling out to the crowd underneath the Gate.

"Oi, you lot, catch a load of this!"

He loosened the string of his plimsoll bag and took out a handful of marbles. By now some of the children had stopped watching John picking up his winnings and had gathered in the Square to see what Raymond was up to.

"You can keep 'em!" Raymond announced and he tossed the handful of marbles into the air.

They bounced and scattered across the Square to be assiduously chased by children to whom marbles were as precious as shells used to be to Andaman Islanders. Handful followed handful and the Square was in uproar. Raymond's bag was soon empty and he went indoors. The scramble for the marbles only lasted a few minutes, but marbles were found in nooks in the Square for days afterwards, some to the annoyance of normally upright adults.

Raymond never played marbles again. He sold the rest of his marble hoard to John at a knock down price and bought a couple of packets of 'Seniors' with the proceeds. John resold them at a premium in dribs and drabs to the rising generation of marbles players.

The story of the great marbles match became a legend that was passed down from one generation of Cottage kids to the next, and to have been one of those who witnessed it was to be envied and admired by all those marble players who came after.

WORK

When Jimmy was seven his mum got a part time job cleaning the offices in one of the clothing factories in Shepherdess Walk. It was there that she got to know the manager of the factory canteen and he offered her the job of tea lady and vegetable cook. She would take the tea trolley around the factory floor and the offices in the morning, prepare and cook the vegetables for lunch under the direction of the canteen manageress, serve the dinners, wash up, and then take the teas round in the afternoon. It was a nine thirty to four job which allowed her to see Jimmy off to school in the morning and to get home half an hour after he did. Usually he would be playing in the Square when she got back. Sometimes she would make a detour to the shops in Essex Road. She rarely asked Jimmy to get her errands. She believed that a child's time was too precious for that.

*

"Your school days are the best days of your life Jimmy." She came out with the old cliché.

Jimmy might have agreed with her if the days did not involve going to school.

"I enjoyed school but I wasn't clever – it seemed as if none of us Hoxton kids were." Mrs. Barton reminisced.

"I used to like drawing as I remember. Mum and dad had no time for education though, especially for us girls. Mum found me a job at 14. I was sent along to the Ardath factory in Old Street to make cigarettes on piecework. The smell of that tobacco used to make me feel sick, and we came out reeking of it. Your Auntie May was already working there; she used to make cigars by hand. All the cigarettes were made by hand as well."

Jimmy visualised his mother rolling cigarettes and licking the papers like he had seen some of the Cottagers doing.

"No Jimmy, I didn't roll them in my fingers, I had to use a see through tube like thing called a 'kirtle' and gather the tobacco up with something we called a 'klonki'."

Jimmy laughed.

"Really Jimmy, that's what they were called, I think, but I can't remember exactly how we did it now. I remember the cigarette papers were already made up into paper tubes, and we would put one in the 'kirtle', push in the tobacco on the 'klonki' and poke the cigarette out with a cut down wooden knitting needle. I made hundreds every day. It was a real sweat shop, and very dreary work as well."

"We used to sit at tables covered with fine metal mesh, gold in colour it was. The forelady used to bring round the tobacco and pile it on to the table. As we worked the tobacco dust would fall through the mesh and it'd be collected up later for making snuff I think. We had to trim the tobacco from the ends of the cigarettes with very sharp scissors, a handful of cigarettes at a time and with one cut; and God help you if you cut into the paper. The forelady would come round to collect the cigarettes, she would weigh them and check for loosely filled ones and look for nicks in the papers. If she found anything she wasn't happy with the cow would screw the lot up and we would have to unpick them and start again. Being on piecework we only got paid for the good ones we had made. If we made too many mistakes we would be out on our ear of course, and there were plenty of girls willing to take our place. I eventually got the hang of it though."

"We used to make 'Kensitas' and 'Black Cat', but the posh cigarettes for the gentry were made by these little bearded Jewish men in skull caps. They made beautiful cigarettes with red silk tips on them, out of Turkish tobacco, and they were packed into silk lined boxes. I think most of them were sent abroad. I hated that job but I put up with it for four years for mum's sake. The smell of the stuff finally drove me out. Mum couldn't believe that I had actually left the factory, I just walked out one day. Nobody walked out of a job in those days."

Martha Barton's face lit up when she told Jimmy about her subsequent career.

"The next day I walked up Kingsland Road to the new Marks and Spencer's opposite Ridley Road market and asked the manager for a job. They were recruiting sales girls then. He looked me up and down. I was only 18. 'Any experience?' he says. I said I hadn't but I told him about the cigarette factory work I'd been doing. 'Have you got a black dress?' he says. 'Yes,' I fibbed. 'Well, bring it along and you can start next week.' I must have run home to mum, I was so pleased. Your Aunt May lent me her new black dress – she had only just finished making it – until I could get my own. I loved that job. I must have been there for about seven years in all, and I became what they used to call a floor walker, making sure that all the counters were fully stocked and keeping an eye out for pilfering and tea leaves, and we caught some too."

"You know I was one of the first Marks and Spencer's girls to sell Walls' ice cream. I had to stand by this ice box

32

by the front doors shouting out 'Walls', they're lovely', and being a coster's daughter I had no problem with that. I did enjoy myself, and I sold loads of the stuff as well. I had to leave Marks' when Sally was due and I never got the chance to go back again what with Sally and then the War. They were good to me there. They gave me some money as a leaving present – and we bought your dad's piano with it."

"The worst job I ever had though was during the War in Todmorden when we were evacuated." Mrs. Barton recalled.

"I thought I was tough coming from Hoxton, but those Yorkshire women in the cotton mills worked as hard as the men, and swore like them too. I couldn't stand the noise in the mill and the cotton in the air, it was worse than in that bloody Ardath factory. They thought I was a soft Southerner. You know Jimmy, the boys up there didn't play like you and your mates do, they used to spend their time kicking at each other's shins with their wooden clogs. I suppose they had to be hard to work the way they did. Give me shop work any day."

*

Of course Jimmy's mum had always done paid work either at home or part–time when this could be fitted in with the daily routine. But her new canteen job at the 'Canda' clothes factory, allowed her to give up for good the work at home that she had been doing on and off since Jimmy was born. For many tedious hours while Jimmy played, and often in the evenings and at weekends too, she would sew buttons on to cards, or fit covers and frills on to lampshades, or stick trouser belts together, or assemble powder puffs, or stuff and sew rag dolls. Every spare corner of the flat in Cornwall Cottages contained cardboard boxes full of the partially finished materials and others full of the finished articles. She carted these boxes back and forth to the local sweatshops, where she collected the couple of shillings per gross that the work was worth. For many of the women with young children down the Street such work was an essential if exploitative cottage industry.

Mrs. Barton disliked jobs involving glue, and belt making was the worst of these. The belts came in two halves and had to be glued together along their full length. Mrs. Barton heated the glue pot on the scullery stove and laid out the belts on the old kitchen table. She spread the hot glue with a brush and smoothed out the conjoined belts on that part of the table that was not yet contaminated with glue. The point was not to get glue on the outside faces of the belts. Jimmy found no little satisfaction in peeling the dried glue from the table top, and for years after his mum had given up belt making he found traces of glue to pick at, especially in the joints between the sadly abused planks of the table top and along its edges. Mrs. Barton only made belts for a short time because of the awful smell of the glue and the disruption it caused to the domestic routine of the household.

Lampshade making was less of an anti–social activity but it also involved glue although a lot less of it than belt making required. Each paper shade was glued into a cone shape, attached to its wire frame and a jolly cotton frill glued along its bottom edge. The demand for lampshades seemed to be insatiable as electricity was brought to more and more Londoners and columns of the things grew taller by the day behind Charlie Barton's armchair. Jimmy was too young to appreciate the irony of his mother making electric lampshades by gaslight.

Martha Barton preferred the homework that involved sewing. Although she had no formal training, apart from needlework at Gopsal Street School, she had always made clothes for herself and her children, and also for neighbours. They had discovered that she hardly ever said no to running up something for them on her pride and joy, a hand operated

Singer sewing machine. Mr. Barton would get exasperated at her easygoing nature. He thought the neighbours took her on, as he put it. Although she did not like being told what she should or should not do, by her husband or anybody else, it was obvious that sometimes she wished that she had refused a sewing job even though she got a few bob for her pains.

Jimmy used to play with the green box of clever Singer sewing machine attachments that his mother had never quite mastered, and with buttons and thimbles and discarded cotton reels while his mother sewed. However he was forbidden to flick the levers or turn the wheel on the sewing machine itself. He would watch in fascination as she positioned the material under the needle, dropped the foot down and started to turn the wheel. The needle would move slowly up and down at first and then become a blur as she rotated the handle more quickly and pushed the material steadily through with her left hand. Whenever she had to turn the wheel back to retrieve the material and unpick an untrue line of stitches she would grumble about not having both hands free. She thought that she would never get used to a treadle machine after years of grinding by hand but she hoped one day to get an electric motor fixed on the old Singer. But the Barton flat was still gas only, even the refrigerator was gas operated.

Electricity had been installed in the refurbished flats on the ground floor of Cornwall Cottages. However it took a while before it eventually reached the top floor and Martha Barton finally got her electric motor, accompanied by complaints from neighbours that it caused 'interference' on the screens of their newly acquired television sets. Even though she then had a 'suppresser' fixed to the motor she never believed that it actually worked, and more often than not she did her sewing on the machine in the old manual way. The 'interference' business did however give her an excuse for refusing the more blatantly mercenary requests for her to run up a dress or to take in a pair of trousers.

As a sideline Martha Barton would also make rag rugs for neighbours as well as for the Barton household. A customer would bring round some good jumble–bought clothes, usually brightly coloured ladies' coats, and she would cut them up into strips about five inches long and one inch wide. Then she would sit with a sheet of hessian, or even a jute onion bag on her lap, and force each strip twice through the hessian using a special pointed tool that also gripped the end of the strip of material. The tool had a spring loaded lever which when pressed with the thumb would open the grip and release the material. She pushed and pulled hundreds of strips through the hessian, side by side, firstly to form the outline frame of the rug usually in one colour, and then to create the centre in a different colour, or in some simple geometric pattern to suit the colours she had available. Her final job was to trim the hessian and turn over a two–inch seam and sew it into position underneath. The rugs were extremely hardwearing and very popular for brightening up the passage and for relieving tired feet in the scullery.

Martha Barton's sweatshop sewing homework however did not involve the use of her sewing machine, but only needle and cotton. The most tedious of these sewing task was the stitching of sets of buttons on to cards for sale in haberdashers' shops. Sometimes as many as 36 blouse buttons would have to be sewn on to one card, or as few as four large fancy coat buttons. The cards were printed with marks indicating the centres of each button and had 'Excelsior' printed in one corner and 'Made In England' in another.

"Made in England isn't the word for it," Jimmy's mum would mutter as she packed the completed cards into the small stout cardboard boxes provided for the purpose. She would drag Jimmy along to Green Man Street where the Button Company had some premises between a malodorous cats' meat shop and a deliciously pungent home made sweet shop. Here she would hand over the boxes of buttons, get new supplies and pick up her meagre wages, and sometimes she would buy a bag of aniseed twist for a treat.

Jimmy also used to help his mother carry voluminous boxes of powder puffs to and from Goswell Road, a round trip of nearly two miles. The powder puff factory had a tiny counter in a room off the street, whose walls had posters announcing that 'Coughs and sneezes spread diseases'. Jimmy had some vague notion that sneezing had something to do with powder puffs, but he never made any logical connection. From the counter Mrs. Barton would box up the week's supplies consisting of soft velvet powder puff cases in several pastel shades, piles of tissue paper faced rounds of cotton wool for stuffing into the cases, and cut lengths of silky ribbon in matching pastel colours. The trips to and from Goswell Road were time consuming but fortunately Mrs. Barton's burdens were not heavy, just bulky. It had been easier when Jimmy was still a baby. She would stack the boxes on top of his pram and check every five minutes to see if he was all right. But he used to sleep through it all.

Each round powder puff case was already machine sewn along most of its twelve–inch circumference with just an inch wide gap showing. Mrs. Barton's first job would be to turn the cases inside out so that the seam was inside and the soft fluffy business side of the powder puff was outside. Then she would push the cotton wool pad through the gap in the stitching without damaging either. Finally she would perform the tricky task of sewing the doubled–over silky ribbon into place at the same time as sewing up the gap itself using a clever stitching method that ensured that no stitches were visible. Boxes with hundreds of pink, blue, yellow, cream and white powder puffs would accumulate in the corners of the front room.

"Jimmy, I don't know what they do with all these bleedin' powder puffs. I wouldn't be surprised if those la–di–da ladies didn't wipe their arses on them," she would laugh and put her needle and cotton down to get the dinner on.

*

Martha Barton's father had been a costermonger. He had a stall for a time on The Waste in Kingsland Road and later in Hoxton Street.

"He was a big man, your grandfather," she recounted to Jimmy as she sewed, "Strong as an ox."

Jimmy's granddad had died two weeks before Jimmy was born in the dreadful winter of 1947.

"The midwife handed you over to me in our bed in the backroom next door and said with a wink 'He's going to be a big one', and all I could think of as I looked at you was 'It's my father, he's been reincarnated'."

Jimmy gave her a look of incomprehension but she continued.

"You know he worked right up to the day he died, he was 75, that bloody winter killed him. I don't know why he carried on so long because I don't think he enjoyed his work particularly. He was always a bit dour and serious and he wouldn't let us kids help him out at all. When I worked at Marks and Spencer's I was full of my new job and I dared to make suggestions about how he could improve the appearance of his stall, lay out potatoes and turnips a bit more artistically, you know, sell some different lines. He wouldn't even call out as the other costers did. I would have done that for him. I would have loved to work with him, but he told me to mind my own business. I think he was a very disappointed man."

"Everyone down Hoxton Market knew Jim Franks, but he kept himself to himself. He used to talk business with the other stallholders but he only had one friend – he was a doctor over in Hyde Road – and dad used to play cards with him and discuss politics I think. He never talked to us about anything though. I would have liked him to show me how to play cards. I still can't play."

"I'll teach you mum," interjected Jimmy, and he had visions of spending long afternoons winning pennies from his mother at 'Chase The Ace'.

"I'm always too busy Jimmy and anyway I don't know 'A' from a bull's foot – that was one of your granddad's sayings, from Canada I think," and she began to tell Jimmy, not for the first time, about the saga of Jim Franks.

"He was teetotal. He never set foot inside a pub, unlike my mum who used to take her peas over to the snug in The Bacchus where she and my little Auntie Alice would sit and shell peas over a glass of stout. I'd pass the pub door sometimes and I'd hear them roaring with laughter. I think the old man signed 'The Pledge' when he was in Canada. That means he promised not to drink Jimmy."

Jimmy was proud and intrigued by the possibility that his grandfather had once been a cowboy.

"No Jimmy, he didn't have a gun, real cowboys couldn't afford them, he used to have a knife; if there was any fighting to be done it was with knives and razors."

Jimmy's granddad had been taken from his family in East London when he was 11 and sent to Canada.

"His mum and dad were skinners by trade, the less you know about them the better, they were terrible drunkards and used to chase each other around the house trying to set each other alight. His brother was too old to be taken into care, it was Barnardos I think, but they sent your granddad out to Canada and indentured him to a bloody Scotch farmer until he was 21. Slavery really. I think he had it tough, they were strict with him, bible punchers, and the non–drinking stuck with him. So Jimmy, he couldn't have been a real cowboy because he didn't go in saloons."

"Why did he come back to England mum? We could have all been Canadian." Jimmy could picture himself lassoing cattle on the Old Chisholm Trail or whatever the equivalent was in Canada.

"Well, when he was 21 he left the farm and went on the tramp. He travelled around Canada, working when he had to, and seeing the country. You know, he knew all about farming, he could handle a team of horses, ride bareback, plough, shoot, chop down trees and punch cattle – they used to punch the beasts with their fists to get them to move, and he had a dislocated knuckle to prove it. So he travelled around, working on farms and ranches and got chummy with another Englishman who was writing to a girl back in London and your granddad began writing to her friend – your grandmother. He came back to Hoxton to get married."

"Why didn't he go back to Canada again mum?" Jimmy wanted to find out why he and his cousins were not riding the range with the Cisco Kid.

"That's why I think he was a disappointed man Jimmy. He wanted to go back to Canada with your grandmother, get a government grant of land and become a farmer himself. But she wouldn't go with him, she was East Ender through and through. He must have been like a fish out of water, 18 years a Canadian countryboy and then he spends the rest of his life as an East End coster. My mum told me that when he first arrived in Hoxton he had a wallet full of money and wore a Stetson hat, but after walking the length of a really bad street he came out at the other end with neither. They didn't steal his independent spirit though. He wouldn't work for anyone. He set himself up with a market stall – my birth certificate says 'occupation of father, master greengrocer'."

"He chewed his 'Pigtail' tobacco and discussed the world over a game of cards with his sawbones friend, and maybe he dreamed of Canada. He had one last adventure though. He sold up his business and joined the army during the First World War. He was accepted even though he was in his forties because he could shoot straight and could handle horses. He went to Mesopotamia to fight the Turks. He came home with nothing, but he set up again selling marrows from the pavement in Hoxton Street. Your granddad wasn't afraid of hard work. I can see him now standing by his stall, his hands black with the cold, flicking off the tiny green shoots from the potatoes with his long thick thumb nail."

*

Jimmy and his dad were passing Rowton House, the great, grim hostel for down and outs behind Mount Pleasant Post Office, and Charlie Barton was instilling his son with the work ethic. They had walked along the streets of Georgian houses that stretched from The Angel to Grays Inn on their way to Doughty Street, which they sometimes did together on those Saturday mornings when the subs were due at the union office. They usually caught a 38 bus back from outside The Yorkshire Grey in Theobalds Road.

Charlie Barton worked in the 'Print'. He sort of drifted into it. When he left Charlie Mutton School in 1924 aged 14 someone got him a job in an engineering shop but it did not suit him. He found what he wanted in a printing shop and enrolled for evening classes at the School of Printing at the Elephant and Castle. For some reason he was not formally apprenticed but nevertheless he stayed the course and became a journeyman printer.

"I must have been about 21 when I got my ticket," Jimmy's dad told him. "When I'd finished with evening classes – I got a certificate of competence as a proper printer's machine minder – they banged me out at work. I'd seen it all before so I knew what to expect. They surrounded me, banging anything to make a noise and smeared me with ink, private parts and all, and paraded me all round the firm for all to see including the girls in the bookbinding room. It took me days to get properly clean again. The Saturday after that our FOC...."

"What's an FOC dad?"

"Father of the Chapel, you know, sort of union shop steward. Anyway he took me down the union offices in Doughty Street. He used to go there one Saturday a month with the dues he collected from our Chapel, just like I'm doing now."

Jimmy was a bit bemused by all these unfamiliar terms but he did not interrupt.

"'Young Charlie 'ere has served his time' he says and I became a full member of the ASLP, that's a real craftsman's union. What does it mean? It stands for The Associated Society of Lithographic Printers Jimmy."

"What does lithographic mean dad?" asked Jimmy now doubly confused.

"Well that's a bit complicated to explain. Let's see, it's a special printing method using zinc plates instead of blocks of letters and engravings. It's quite an old idea, they used to use stone blocks, but today it's all tied up with photography. Whatever has to be printed is photographed and the negative is transferred on to a sensitised zinc plate, which is shaped to fit the rollers of the printing machine. Plate making is a separate job – very skilled. Anyway these plates are sensitive to water. A damper roller on the machine wets the plate but the water only sticks to the places that aren't going to be printed. Another roller then inks the plate and the ink only sticks to the places where it is not damp – the bits that have to be printed. The plate roller and the paper roller then print the picture or whatever it is, on to the paper. Clever eh. Of course it's a lot more complicated than that, especially with colour printing."

Jimmy only half understood what his father was saying.

"Most everyday printing is done on letterpress machines but if they want real quality they call in the Litho boys. We're only a small union, but we're the best. There were only half a dozen of us in the litho department when I was banged out, but where I work now it's all litho."

Charlie Barton worked in a small litho shop in Kentish Town where he printed sheet music, thousands of copies of the latest popular songs from Tin Pan Alley. He used to bring home examples of his art, just four sides of print that cost an exorbitant shilling a song but unfortunately neither he nor Sally could read music. However Jimmy found them useful. Paul Creasey, who lived in one of the ground floor refurbished and enlarged flats that actually had a bathroom, was learning to play the accordion and Jimmy was delighted to swap his dad's sheet music for Paul's comics. The sheets also provided Jimmy with the words of a few of his favourite pop songs including 'Teddy Bear', which he republished, illegally, in his own newspaper. He used a 'John Bull' printing outfit that his father had bought for his birthday. There was only one edition of the paper and only one copy of that. His family had to pay a penny to read it, which was very poor value because it mainly consisted of the words of Elvis's big hit of 1957, which everybody knew anyway by the time Jimmy's paper hit the Street.

Mr. Barton did the honours as FOC at his litho shop, collecting the subs and taking them to the ASLP office. His union duties did not extend much further than this, as unlike the newspaper industry the litho business was hardly ever involved in industrial disputes. The union negotiated the wages with the printing employers, it was a closed shop, and everybody seemed satisfied. Charlie Barton could have earned more in the troubled newspaper business – everyone knew you could get a good screw in the 'Print' – but he was not interested. He enjoyed working in a small intimate workshop where he knew the governor well. In fact his job there was kept open for him all through the war and when he was demobbed he picked up from where he had left off.

"It's not heavy work really. Once I've washed down the rollers and set up the machine, clamped on the plate, seen that the paper is properly loaded in the automatic feeder, done a few runs to get the pressure right, the ink flow right and the plate lined up right – this is really important in colour work because there's a different plate for each colour and the markers have to line up exactly – then I press the green button and the machine does the rest. I just have to keep my eye on things and potter around with my oil can and an oily rag. My NATSOPA mate, that's the printers' assistants' union, he does all the fetching, carrying and bundling up, there'd be trouble if I did his job as well as mine. So with a long run, a couple of thousand copies say, I can relax a bit. Of course if anything goes wrong I have to deal with it. I can fix most things but sometimes we have to call in the engineers. But these Swiss and Italian machines are pretty good and anyway I look after them well enough."

Jimmy and his dad got off the 38 bus at the top of the Street and made their way to Cornwall Cottages.

"What would you like to work at when you grow up Jimmy?" his dad asked as they walked into the passage of their flat.

"I wouldn't mind being a carpenter," said Jimmy.

"Just don't become an insurance man," joined in Mrs. Barton, "I've been stuck in here half the morning waiting for the blighters to turn up for their money, and I haven't even been down the shops yet." She left them with the insurance books, four piles of coins and instructions about who got what, put her coat on and left them to it.

VISITORS

Most nights the gang would meet in the Airey between Cornwall and Queens Cottages. Nobody ever went there after dark except the occasional kid playing runouts. An extraordinary gang meeting had been called for this particular still summer night and Monty, who was the leader of the gang, was late. The other gang members were lounging about on the railings and on the window cills of the empty flat which had once been used for storing building materials when the landlord had unfulfilled ambitions of converting the Cottages into flats with bath rooms.

Monty came loping into the Airey (see illustration 8) from the Cornwall side. He was long and lean and his left eye was pure white. It had been put out in a fight several years before. The fur on his head was rough and tufted from the numerous scratches, digs and bruises he had suffered in his violent rise to feline supremacy in the Cottages. Monty had been a stray for many years ever since his owners had moved away from the Street. They had not named him after the heroic Montgomery, or after the exotic Montezuma, but they had called him Montelimar because he had been such a sweet tabby kitten. Monty had spent his alley cat years living down his domesticated origins and none of the other cats in the gang referred to him by his full name. He was Monty to them and Old One Eye to the Cottagers.

The extraordinary meeting had been called to agree a plan of action regarding a certain individual in whom Monty, and every other cat in the Cottages, had a consuming interest. Monty saw the downfall of this individual as the culmination of his leadership of the gang. His plan was simple. He had spent the evening working it out and now he was ready to enlighten his impatient conspirators. The cats' eyes reflected the light from the solitary lamp in the Airey as they turned to Monty in anticipation. As a formality Monty dealt a couple of padded blows at two of his lieutenants just to let the gang know who was boss, and then he outlined the strategy which would ensure that the individual in question would receive his come–uppance.

The plan, consisting of a two pronged assault involving close pursuit followed by an ambush, was explained to the motley mixture of strays and pampered cats out on the tiles, which made up Monty's gang. The pursuit would not arouse any suspicion, as pursuit would be expected, but at the crucial moment, and in a place chosen by Monty as the most promising, the ambush would be launched. If the plan succeeded it would be up to every cat to grab what he could for himself and to scarper before there was any chance of retaliation.

The meeting was broken up by the homecoming of a Cornwall Cottager whose ground floor flat opened into the short alley that connected the Square to the Airey. The twenty pairs of eyes that gleamed at him out of the darkness beyond the railings were a familiar phenomenon, semi–inebriation notwithstanding.

"Clear off. Shoo. Bloody cats pissing up the doorstep. Piss off out of it."

The eyes switched off and the cats scattered. Monty reassembled a cohort on an access balcony on the Queens side. He led it down into the Square to stalk the brick rubbish boxes situated at the bottom of the chutes serving each block, for a mouse or a rat. They were lucky and found one of the steel sliding doors wedged open with rubbish, which allowed a thorough exploration inside for bones and old sardine tins. The hunt was half hearted because most of the cats were distractedly thinking about their leader's plan of campaign which was to be put into action the following day as soon as their quarry had entered the Cornwall Gate.

Steve would make deliveries down the Street twice a week, on Mondays and Thursdays. He worked from a shop in Greenman Street and every day he filled up his huge basket, hooked the handle over his arm and carried the not inconsiderable load from street to street.

Steve was a heavy thickset man of middle age with strong muscular arms and legs. His black greasy hair was combed back severely, but a pendulous curl was always bouncing on his forehead. For a heavy man he could move quickly and he did his rounds at a lick. The only clean thing about Steve was the big white napkin that covered his basket. His jacket was old and torn, shiny with accumulated grease around the sleeves and lapels. A blood stained butcher's apron concealed the front of his baggy flannels, which were even more disgraceful than his jacket. On his feet he wore a strong pair of trusty Billingsgate boots with steel tips to the toes and heels, and with shiny steel toecaps devoid of their covering of leather.

There was no denying that Steve was an unattractive prospect. And he smelled pretty badly as well. His pungent odour preceded his arrival in the Square. He stamped his way around the balconies giving the occasional cry of 'Cat's Me–eat', and left little packages of cats' delight with those Cottagers who had an arrangement with him. He also sold his wares to the passing trade as he went.

Steve could not hide the nature of his business even if he had wanted to. There was no disguising the presence of horseflesh, huge slabs of which could be seen hanging in the window of his unsavoury premises. The smell of the meat penetrated to the very soul of Steve the Cats' Meat Man and it could be detected by any cat from a hundred yards.

On his rounds through the Cottages Steve would be accompanied by a crowd of mewing cats, absolutely mesmerised by the smell of the tantalising packages hidden under the spotless napkin covering his basket. With tails erect the cats would trot along behind him, to the side of him and sometimes in front of him. Collisions and squabbles would arise among his followers as Steve led them in Pied Piper fashion up and down the open staircases and along the balconies, gathering more as he went. Occasionally a cat would be overcome with frenzied desire and leap up at the basket, but Steve was quick with cuff and boot and kept good order. But he was careful not to abuse his customer's cats, and would aim his blows only at the scruffy, hard bitten strays like Monty and his lieutenants, whom he knew by sight.

Steve's packages consisted of small pieces of meat wrapped tightly and skilfully in newspaper, and of selected delicacies on wooden skewers also wrapped in paper. Some Cottagers would be there to take in the delivery, but mostly Steve would place his packages under the heavy black iron knockers of his customer's doors, infuriatingly out of reach of his followers some of whom would leap up and try to reach the knockers in their intoxication. As Steve stood at doors, free hand delving under the napkin, his legs would be assaulted by adoring cats rubbing their faces and flanks over his deliciously odorous boots and turnups. The cats were ambivalent towards Steve, he was both provider and tormentor, but for Monty and the strays in his gang, Steve was fair game.

On the Monday morning after the gang meeting, Monty's plan was put into action. Lookouts in Edinburgh Cottages had spotted the cats' meat man doing his rounds accompanied by the local Edinburgh cats, which were in a rival gang to Monty's. Word was passed back to Monty that Steve had left Edinburgh and was making his way down the Street. The few Edinburgh cats who stayed with him turned tail when the first of Monty's pursuit troopers ran up to escort Steve into the Cornwall Gate.

The pursuit troopers consisted entirely of well–groomed home loving cats on their best behaviour. While all of the flea bitten strays in the gang were dragooned into the ambush party and on this day they were forbidden to join Steve's perambulation through the Cornwall Gate.

Monty's strategy was to lull Steve into dropping his guard and then to launch a surprise attack. The assault was to take place inside the Gate near the right–hand stairs next to the Doolan residence. Monty knew Steve's routine. He would deliver to the ground floor flats first, to lessen his burden before going up the stairs, and he would always go round in a clockwise direction as a natural consequence of carrying the basket on his right arm, and delivering the packages with his left. Monty knew that Steve would soon be passing the staircase under which he had positioned half of his ambush party. Here the cats hid in the shadows and lurked beneath the two motorbikes, which the Collins brothers always parked there and which were regularly sprayed to let everyone know that this was Monty's parish. The rest of the ambush party was scattered around the Gate and nearby in the Square, wherever a cat could feel inconspicuous.

Steve's steel tipped boots rang out hollowly as he left the Street and entered the Gate. His entourage immediately grew to fifteen and consisted entirely of Monty's well behaved pursuit troops. The cats kept close to Steve's feet but did nothing to disturb his even progress. Steve did not need to reprimand any cat and was hardly aware of their presence until he reached the staircase. Monty gave the signal and the ambush was sprung.

The cats in attendance clawed at Steve's trousers and those hiding beneath the stairs leaped up at his basket. Those with further to run took flying leaps in the direction of the stricken cat's meat man who, caught off guard, stumbled and sat down heavily where the steel string of the staircase met the ground. The napkin covering the basket flapped over to reveal the contents, some of which had spilled on to the floor. Steve kicked out and cuffed as best he could from his sitting position, and at the same time attempted to stand up, retrieve his spillages and secure the basket from Monty's marauders. But the main chance was with the cats. As Monty had explained it was every cat for himself and those that managed to grab a package ran off with it to safer ground. It was all over in seconds. Steve was back on his feet. His basket was securely hooked over his arm but minus half a dozen meal–sized portions of packaged horsemeat. He was a bit shaken, more by the audacity of the Cornwall cats than by any physical discomfort. However both he and the cats knew that this was a one off enterprise, one that could never be repeated.

Monty dashed off to the Airey with his prize and ate the meat in its cool seclusion. He had realised two ambitions. His long–term tormentor had been ridiculed and now for the first time he had tasted Steve's wares. He spent the rest of the day sunning himself and dozing on the railings of the top balcony of Cornwall Cottages. The familiar flap of the washing, which was strung across the corners of the Square from railing to railing, was all that disturbed his ruminations on the morning's events. He had feasted on Steve's finest, but it had left him with the cloying aftertaste of long forgotten domesticity. But he had got Steve out of his system and now he looked forward to the coming night when he would lead his gang in the search for more exotic, fur wrapped viands in the darker places of the Cottages.

*

Steve the Cats' Meat Man was only one of the many visitors who came collecting and selling or delivering to the Cottagers. Some wore suits including the rent man, the insurance men and the tallymen from the few departmental stores that gave credit. Some wore uniforms such as the gasman and the milk man while others came in their work clothes such as the coal man and the chimney sweep, and Steve of course.

Of the regular visitors the one most welcomed by the Cottagers was the gas man because he always left a refund from the money that had been fed into the gas meter over the previous months.

Jimmy's mother would answer the man's confident knock and he would step into the passage of the flat without waiting for an invitation. He knew where the meter was situated, high in the corner of the front room over the 'Put–U–Up', it's utilitarian nakedness hidden by a short ruffled curtain on a piece of wire. The man worked at remarkable speed. From his satchel he would produce a huge bundle of keys, which were attached to his belt by a long chain and open the padlock to the collecting box situated on the side of the meter. He would lift the metal box gingerly down and place it on the dining table and then check the meter reading. He would make a note of the reading in his duplicate book and then tip the coins out of the box on to the table. Jimmy would watch in absorbed silence as the gas man spread the shilling coins over the table and then slide them off the edge with lightning fingers into his waiting hand, counting as he went. At twenty he would stand a neat column of coins upright on the table with a clack. After a few seconds there would be up to ten columns of shillings depending on the season,

51

laid out in rows like a Greek antiquity. The gasman would then delve into his satchel to produce strong brown paper envelopes marked '£5' into which most of the coins would disappear and he would pencil a note on them to remind him how much they contained. He would fold down the openings to the envelopes tightly and stash the money away in the bottom of his satchel. He would then fit the collecting box and its padlock back on to the meter.

Now would came the moment that Jimmy had been anticipating. The gasman would calculate the cost of the gas used from the meter reading and compare it with the money collected. He would make a note in his duplicate book and tear off the top copy as a receipt. This together with the refund would be ceremoniously laid on the table and the gasman would let himself out. Jimmy would count the little pile of coins and take them to his mother. She would let him keep the coppers and get him to put a couple of shillings back in the meter. He would stand on the head rest and the arm of the 'Put–U–Up' and stretch up to the gas meter. After twisting back the stiff brass handle, the slot for the shilling coins would be revealed. The coins would fall noisily into the empty box, securing the gas supply for another few days, and would stay there until the gasman returned. It was a relief when the gas meter had been emptied because temptation was also removed from those criminally inclined Cottages' who sometimes had it away with their neighbours' gas meter boxes when money was scarce.

Wally the Paperboy and his wife Lil had a virtual monopoly on newspaper sales in the Cottages. They had a stall at the top of the Street where it joined Essex Road, right outside the Half Moon. From there they organised their early morning deliveries, and sold newspapers, magazines and comics during the day. Wally also had a job as a part time fireman in the afternoons. If there had been more hours in the day they would have sold evening papers as well, but they let this business opportunity lapse in favour of sleep. The Cottagers believed that Wally and Lil had plenty of money, even though their appearance gave no support to this hypothesis. They were the worst dressed people down the Street.

They both wore flat caps and threadbare overcoats tied around the middle with string. She wore men's shoes and trousers and woollen gloves with the fingertips missing. Their hands and faces were usually ground in with newsprint and they worked like Trojans, especially on Sunday mornings when their grown up son would also help out with the deliveries. On weekdays they would have completed their rounds before seven o'clock, but on Sundays late rising Cottagers would be able to spot them still shuffling around the balconies toting swollen canvas satchels with 'Evening News' stencilled on the side, and sniping at each other. And in the middle of the Square their parked box cart, home made out of four by twos, pram wheels and plywood, was filled to the gunnels with 'News of The World's'.

In summertime of course the ice cream man used to visit. He worked for the 'Daily Ice Cream Co.' and rode a tricycle with a huge green box on the front with four silver circular lids on the top. The box was full of ice–lollies and individual cardboard tubs of ice cream, green and cubic like the tricycle box. Word would reach the Cornwall kids that the ice cream man was outside Edinburgh and was coming down the Street. Some of the children had money on them and others ran home to get some. Jimmy would shout out from the Square up to the door of his flat on the top balcony desparately trying to attract his mother's attention. He knew from experience that if she had the radio on she might not hear him and if he ran upstairs to get some money he might be too late and the Daily Ice Cream man would be half way down Packington Street by the time he got to the Gate again. Either way Jimmy's mum was usually forthcoming with thrupence. If she heard him she would screw up the coins in a brown paper bag and drop it into the Square. Jimmy would retrieve the money and run out to the Gate.

At one time the Daily Ice Cream man used to hand out cards with pictures of locomotives on them, but there were only a few in the set and 'Daily' never introduced another. The children down the Street had hundreds of cards all the same, just right for flicking up the wall. There was also an abundance of discarded lolly sticks around when the ice cream man had been. A regular summertime fad among the children was weaving lolly sticks together like miniature wany fence panels, which they used to make rafts and stockades for their battered toy cowboys and soldiers.

Jimmy's mother loved ice cream and would sometimes ask him to bring her one up also. "Course, it's not like the ice cream when I was a girl," she would say as they dug into the small green boxes with the flat wooden spoons. "Our dad's house in Hoxton was right next door to an Italian ice cream man. He used to make his own. It was called 'Hokey Pokey'. We used to watch him make it in his back yard sometimes. He had a contraption, all clean and shiny it was, a bit like a milk churn. It had a tub on the inside, and he used to pack ice around it, but he put all the ingredients inside the tub. Nothing but the best mind. Eggs and milk and sugar and sticks of vanilla. He would screw the lid down and turn the handle. When the handle got stiff to turn he checked to see how the ice cream was doing. It would form around the sides of the tub. Lovely it was. He used to sell it around the streets. 'Hokey Pokey, penny a lump, the more you eat the more you jump'. That's what he used to call out. You don't see it anymore. That was before the war."

*

On Sunday afternoons, just as the pubs were closing the winkle man would wheel his coster's barrow into the

Square. He was a short thickset young man with striking blonde hair and blue eyes, and a clubfoot, which hardly slowed him down at all, and he wore a long white coat. His barrow was well stocked with fruits–de–mer for Sunday tea with bread and butter. He had shrimps, prawns, winkles, cockles, mussels, whelks and jellied eels and he measured them out in a couple of half pint and pint pewter pots. As he entered each Square the winkle man would yell out of the corner of his mouth an unintelligible 'Shrim's–an–win'yar–alls', which rose to a long held crescendo on the 'yar' part. He was merely calling out 'Shrimps and winkles' but it had become distorted in the effort of getting his presence known to the Cottagers before they settled down to their Sunday naps. Jimmy would be sent down to get his dad half a pint of winkles for his tea. The winkle man would reach for the pot, which was perched on the mound of winkles and dig deep into the shells, which would clatter noisily over each other. He would rip off a brown paper bag from the string nailed to the side of the barrow and upend the pot of winkles into it, followed immediately by half a handful for good measure.

Jimmy would watch his father later in the evening lifting the lids off each winkle with a pin and delving inside to pull out perfectly curled black springy objects, which he would liberally powder with pepper, and down with bites of bread and 'Stork' (he did not like butter), and mouthfuls of tea. Mr Barton sometimes tried to get Jimmy interested in the delights of molluscs and crustaceans but Jimmy thought they were disgusting. His mother said he was a finick.

Other regular visitors to the Square included the rag and bone man and the knife grinder with his pedal powered grindwheeling bicycle, and occasionally in the summer a Romany would give rides to children on his pony and trap. The most poignant of the visitors to the Square however were the street singers.

The Square made an ideal auditorium for a solo singing performance, a bit like the courtyard of a coaching inn when used by a travelling Elizabethan theatre, but the performances were hardly comparable. The singer, in great coat and working boots would clap one hand over his ear and hang on to his cloth cap with the other, and belt out a pre–war sentimental song. Jimmy's mum always got him to throw a few coppers down from the balcony and the Square would ring as other Cottagers made their contributions, some of which were thrown a bit harder than was necessary. The man would sing an encore before collecting up his money and then move on to the next Square.

*

"I hate to see that," Jimmy's mother would say, "Probably an old soldier down on his luck. Course it's begging really. Against the law I suppose. But I hate to see them losing their dignity like that. It was worse after that bloody first war. They used to sing down Hoxton market, young men, unemployed, and some of them with only one arm or leg or half blinded. It really used to upset me as a girl. Your granddad came back from that war with nothing as well. But he managed to carry on where he left off, selling vegetables in the market. He started up again by walking to Spitalfields and bringing back a sack of marrows on his head. He laid them out in the street and sold them, and then he walked back to Spitalfields for some more. He always found a few pennies to give to those poor buggers."

MONDAY TO FRIDAY

Charlie Barton would already be in Kentish Town with his overalls on fresh from the laundry and his offset printing machine running when Jimmy got up to go to school. His sister Sally would also be well on her way to Piccadilly where she worked as a short hand typist for a firm of solicitors. His mum would make him some toast and badger him to get washed and dressed. On winter mornings he would sit cross–legged on the floor in his underwear, his back freezing and his shins roasting in front of the one bar electric fire, in a semi–catatonic state, unable to move until his toast arrived. Martha Barton would watch her son reluctantly disappear out of the Gate. She would tidy up, put her coat on, and then go into the bedroom. She would lift the bottom sash and lean out of the window in time to see him join the crowd at the bottom of Pickering Street outside the gate of the boys' playground of Charlie Mutton Junior Mixed. He would wave and she would wave back, now she could go to work as well.

Charlie Mutton's was a typical two storey red brick Edwardian LCC school, with very tall bright classrooms lit by huge windows, which were opened with long poles kept on brackets above magnificent cast iron radiators. It had two playgrounds on either side of the main school building, one for boys and the other for girls. Each playground had dingy outside toilets and an undercroft area where the scholars could shelter from bad weather. The walls of Charlie Mutton School were being steadily undermined by the depredations of generations of boys who had scraped out dozens of semi–circular holes in the soft red bricks using penny coins. These would be given superb coppery shines with the resultant red brick dust and spit. The walls in the girl's playground however had more prosaic uses. The girls would do handstands and play two or three balls up the wall.

Jimmy was in Miss Steifle's class, and unusually she had kept with the same group of 40 children, of whom Jimmy was one, for three years running as they passed through the Charlie Mutton mincer. She kept a big tin of Lincoln biscuits on the window cill and would dole them out to the children at two for an (unshined) penny to go with their morning bottle of milk. He liked his teacher. He was one of her eleven plus hopefuls, and she had given him a lot of encouragement especially in writing compositions as they were called.

Miss Steifle was a buxom middle aged blonde woman and still rather pretty. She had lost someone special when the Bismarck sank the Hood during the war. She would teach Jimmy's class for every lesson except handicraft but including the dreaded Country Dancing at which she would pick up any reluctant boy, Jimmy was one, and make him dance with her. She would lift him off the floor as she whirled him around the school hall. Even those boys who contrived to wear Wellington boots for the occasion would not be spared the embarrassment. The girls in the class thought that Country Dancing in the school hall was great fun.

The hall was of course used for morning assembly but there was a time when Jimmy was excused from attending. At one of the hated school medical examinations the doctor had found something wrong with his feet. Apparently they were not the only dodgy pair in the school because he had to join a group of other pupils for foot exercises at assembly time. It had seemed strange to him that while his classmates were destroying 'All Things Bright and Beautiful', he was learning how to hold a pencil with his toes and to draw pictures with it. He grew to enjoy these sessions especially if they included team hopping races in which small balls or bean bags were passed from the foot of one team member to the next in relay. He never knew what was wrong with his feet or whether the exercises made any difference, he only knew that one day the sessions stopped and he was back in the hall singing 'Onward Christian Soldiers'

Jimmy was not a natural scholar but he enjoyed his schoolwork. He found that he had a knack for accumulating general knowledge, gleaned from the back pages of 'The Topper' and 'The Beezer' and from cigarette cards. He would regurgitate this knowledge at school at every opportunity. He had once emphatically declared in an English composition that the rhinoceros' horn was full of compressed air, and no one had contradicted him. It was many years later that he realised what a ludicrous notion this was, and that the rhino's terrible pneumatic horn was not inflatable at all but was actually made of compressed hair. Jimmy's stock of useless information meant that he would often be consulted by friends in the Cottages about the ways of the world and was sometimes asked to arbitrate in disputes. At school however he was not as popular as he was at home. Most of his classmates did not live in the Cottages, in fact only three girls and one other boy did so, and also he did not normally mix with classmates outside of the school playground. In fact he had no close friends at Charlie Mutton's at all, apart from Alan who was in the year below him and that did not count.

Despite being the fount of useless knowledge Jimmy was shy and self conscious among people he did not know well. Towards the end of his four years at Charlie Mutton Junior Mixed he had become overweight and conscious of it to such an extent that he kept his jacket on in class. And he would sidle crab like along the walls of the corridors and classrooms so that people could not look at his posterior. Nobody ever asked him about this curious but fortunately short lived behaviour, perhaps they never noticed. Being self conscious was also the reason for his hatred of medical examinations. It was bad enough having to stand in front of the doctor and the 'Nitty Nora' in only your underpants with the other boys in the line looking at your bum and probably sniggering. But there was always another woman there who just stood ominously to one side grinning and never saying a word. What horrible impairment she was looking out for to embarrass him with, Jimmy had dreaded to speculate. She had an extremely unfortunate face, like a smacked arse, as Jimmy's mum would say. She wore a grey uniform with a Baden Powell style hat, and she had something to do with the church or so Jimmy surmised. He had seen her a few times at Sunday school in St. James' church hall in Britannia Row. If he came across her in the street his heart would sink as he was instantly reminded of the embarrassing prospect and certainty of yet another medical examination in the future. God knows who she was.

A short stint at Sunday school was only a hiccough in his otherwise non–religious upbringing. Apart from school assembly and the nightly thought prayer that his mother had taught him when he was tiny, the one that goes 'Now I lay me down to sleep', he had no contact with Christianity, despite his maiden aunts having Holy Water. But in order to join the Wolf Cubs he had to attend Sunday school, which was as much a novelty to him as the Cubs meetings were. Inevitably he grew tired of both but he might have persevered had the St. James' pack not been disbanded due to lack of support shortly after the Jubilee Jamboree. He could have joined the neighbouring pack in Vincent Terrace but it would have meant going alone deep into alien territory, in uniform, and also none of his friends from the Street had joined, they would not have been seen dead in the Cubs. While it lasted he had enjoyed the experience, sitting in a circle in St. James' church hall eating sausages, mash and baked beans, chanting DOB, DOB, DOB in answer to the 'sixer's' DYB, DYB, DYB, leaping up and down with his hands on his head like a wolf and shouting to Arkela 'Arkela we'll do our best', and partaking in the 'Grand Howl'. He had experienced the kind of camaraderie he had not felt since 'foot classes' at school. He even earned one or two badges for the uniform that his long–suffering mother had bought for him. He realised later that he had been caught up in the short–lived surge of interest in the Scouts and Cubs that accompanied the 50th Anniversary celebrations of Baden Powell's founding of the Boy Scout movement. Indeed Jimmy Barton had been there with his cub pack in the grand Jubilee Jamboree parade that marched up Holloway Road one Sunday morning in 1957, and he still has the specially issued brass woggle to prove it.

Jimmy's desperate self–consciousness was the reason he never learned to swim while at Charlie Mutton's. The swimming baths at The 'Tib' were only five minutes away in Greenman Street and lessons were held there all year round, but they were not compulsory, to his great relief, and he declined the opportunity to learn there. He could not easily hide his bottom from view in a public swimming pool and also he was certain that he would be a dead loss at swimming, as he appeared to be at all sports. His self–consciousness was accompanied by a great fear of humiliation.

Although he was competent enough at Street games he was not good at regular sports and he became more and more athletically gauche as he passed through the school. He found the occasional football trials he was forced to partake in on the terrible cinder pitches at Finsbury Park some of the most dispiriting of his school experiences. However he did enjoy the underground trip from Essex Road tube station. The only sporting skill he possessed was the ability to throw stones accurately, a skill he had honed on the bomb ruins, but stone throwing was not on the school curriculum. He became useless at team games not only because of his lack of skill but also because of his dislike of physical contact and because of his empathy for those who lost. At first he had wanted to play football and cricket and run races but he had no instinct for it and completely the wrong attitude, and eventually he grew tired of being ineffectual and of not being picked for playground teams. As his friends and classmates grew in confidence he convinced himself that sport held no interest for him either as a participant or as a spectator. Charlie Barton had not introduced his son to the joys of sport as he himself only took a sporadic interest in professional boxing and had never expressed any interest at all in football and cricket. But what his dad did or did not do had no influence on the matter, Jimmy Barton just did not have that feeling for sport which seemed to come naturally to other boys.

His dislike of serious sport, as opposed to the Street games that he loved, and his fear of medical examinations and the swimming baths were accompanied by two other dreads which were more rationally based. He feared the school dentist whose ghastly instruments of torment occupied a room above the school treatment centre. It was next to Budding's, the sweet shop that was one of the causes of Jimmy's dental problems, the other being Albert's the only shop in Popham Street. He would grimace and look away every time he walked past the stairs leading up to the dental surgery. On a couple of visits with his mum, his teeth had been painfully filled and one or two baby teeth had been removed after the application of an evil smelling rubber gas mask. The treatment room below was a lot less dreadful but it still evoked memories of cuts and grazes dealt with unsympathetically by a disinfectant–wielding nurse. She would lift the invalid on to the big central table and tell him not to be a baby as he winced to the sting of the iodine that turned his knee indigo blue. The limp back to school was soon followed by a boisterous time in the playground where it seemed that every tenth child displayed a purple knee or elbow.

Jimmy also dreaded encounters with bullies whom he assiduously avoided. Miss Steifle's class was free of bullies, although one or two boys were friends with the tough guys in the other class of Jimmy's year. The toughest boys mostly came from the Street, the lower end around Albany Cottages, but they tolerated him, probably because he was a Street kid like them. However if he ever felt anything but ignored by the bullies he would go home the long way round – up Pickering Street to Essex Road and down the Street from the Half Moon end. Sometimes he would take an unorthodox short cut from Pickering Street around the top end of the Cornwall Cottages block where there was a small bomb ruins backing on to the bedrooms of the offset block of Edinburgh Cottages. If he climbed a wall and some railings and took a chance at being spotted by a policeman, a caretaker or an interfering Cottager, he could reach the dank Airey separating Edinburgh from Cornwall Cottages. After using this short cut a couple of times the adventure of it wore off and he hardly ever went there again, although it was good to know about it, in case of emergencies.

On his way home from school Jimmy would often join the kids buying sweets in Albert's shop which occupied the only house in the Street to be spared by the Luftwaffe. They never bought wholesome confectionery; they could not afford it anyway. They bought junk as dictated by the latest fads – multi–layered multi–coloured gob stoppers, aniseed balls, lemonade powder sucked from their fingers which then turned bright orange, liquorice, sherbet filled flying saucers, black jack chews, banana and chocolate flavoured slabs of 'Palm' toffee, thick teeth bending penny chews, awful shrimp shaped pink and perfumed dollops of congealed goo, choking sherbet 'fountains' with liquorice straws, tubes of 'Love Hearts', 'Refreshers' and 'Spangles', and of course bubble gum which often came with picture cards that could be collected or swapped. Jimmy spent a lot of pocket money trying to get 'Colombia', the only flag in the 'Flags of The World' series that he did not have. He had no idea where Colombia was but he knew that if he got it, like Terry, he could give up buying the awful bubble gum. God knows what was in all these childhood delights but one thing was certain, they made a lot of business for the school dentist.

In summer of course everybody bought ice–lollies. Jimmy's particular favourite was called 'Everest'. It was a pyramid of creamy ice on a stick with card wrapped around four of its five sides. The ice was soft on the tongue, not solid rock like some lollies, and sometimes the tip of the pyramid would break off when the wrapper was removed. The pyramid could be sculpted using the tip of the tongue to make a small Henry Mooreish maquette, which could fit into the mouth all at once. Ecstasy, especially if it was a lemon one.

Sometimes Jimmy had to go home from school via the bag wash shop, which was down the Bottom between Budding's and the school treatment centre. At one time his mum had washed the Barton's laundry in the wash house at the 'Tib', but with working almost full time she would use the bag wash laundry instead, however she would still wash some things at home. The shop had a clean damp smell about it, which was not surprising, because two walls were lined with canvas sacks filled with freshly washed clothes, stacked floor to ceiling on timber racking. Jimmy would produce the laundry ticket and the laundry woman would match it to a wet sack and heave this on to the counter. Jimmy would hand over the coins and lift the bag wash on to his shoulder and carry it home without getting his clothes too damp. If it were heavier or wetter than usual he would swing the bag along the pavement as best he could. He much preferred taking the bag down to the shop when it was dry and appreciably lighter. Sometimes when the bag was emptied, Mrs. Barton would discover a sock or a pair of knickers that belonged to somebody else, or worse she would discover that a sock or pair of knickers was missing. The bag wash shop operated a rather ineffective lost and found service. It never occurred to Jimmy until many years later that the dirty clothes were actually taken out of the bag to be washed, which explained the mystery of how the washing got mixed up in the bags. He had always assumed that as the bag was wet when it was collected it had been washed, as it was, full and unopened, and pummelled and squeezed by some infernal laundry machine.

As soon as she had a moment Jimmy's mum would undo the wire around the neck of the bag wash and empty the contents on to the swept passage lino, and then peg out the washing piece by piece on the line strung across the Cornwall Square (See illustrations 5 and 7). All the balconies supported washing lines, and there was hardly ever a dry day without several bag loads of clothes flapping in most of the four corners of the Square. Each line ran in a knotted loop between two galvanised iron pulleys tied to the top rails of the balustrades. Several lines, belonging to different Cottagers, crossed the void side by side, not necessarily parallel, and far enough apart to stop the washing becoming entangled. The lines decreased in length the nearer they were to the corner where they were often duplicated to provide sufficient capacity for a bag wash load.

*

"Bring out the rest will you Jimmy?" Mrs. Barton asked as he stood next to her on the balcony.

He was staring down into the empty Square in the hope of seeing one of his friends materialise.

"The washing Jimmy," she said in exasperation.

He dragged himself away from the railings and distractedly brought the last of the wet towels out from the passage and draped them over his arms so that his mother could peg them on the line. She pulled the upper part of the line towards her and the bottom part moved the hanging washing out into space, and revealed a free length of line for the next piece of washing. The pulleys gave out squeals of protest. Each pulley had its own range of frequencies and decibel rating. When it rained Cottagers would dash out to retrieve their par–dried washing and set up a teeth grinding cacophony of squeaks and squeals resounding round the balconies.

"Is this the last of it Jimmy," Mrs. Barton asked as she took a wiping up cloth from him.

He grunted. She pulled the heavily laden line across the Square a little further but she had not been taking note of the situation at the far end of the line. The peg holding up the shoulder of one of Jimmy's school jerseys was drawn into the far pulley, and was pinged off. The wet jersey swung away, pulling the other peg with it, and it fell into the Square three storeys below.

"Sugar, sugar, sugar, sugar!" said Mrs. Barton, followed immediately by "Shit, shit, shit!" as well she might as there were probably samples of both kinds of expletives among the detritus that kids, cats, dogs and sloppy dustmen had left for the wind and rain to pursue around the Square.

"Would you run down and get that for me, there's a dear?"

"OK mum." Jimmy sloped off down the stairs and picked his jersey out of the smattering of potato peelings near the door of the dustbin enclosure at the bottom of the rubbish chute, and hunted around for the pegs.

"You can't wear this now, look at it," Jimmy's mum held up his best jersey and examined the dirt of unknown origin adhering to it, "Put it in the bath love and I'll wash it out later."

It was inevitable that clothes and pegs ended up in the Square, as did whole washing lines together with their pendulous loads if a line snapped or came undone. Jimmy dropped his jersey into the upended tin bath that lurked behind the scullery door, and it slid on to the floor, as expected. He went back on to the balcony and spotted Terry crossing the Square.

"Hey, Tel, where'ya going? He hollered over the balcony.

Mrs. Barton gave a jump.

"Don't shout like that, there's babies trying to sleep."

"Down the chip shop – me Nan's forgot to buy me tea," Terry yelled up from below.

"Hang on, I'll come with ya." Jimmy looked at his mum, she nodded and he ran around to the stairs.

She looked at him disparagingly as he reached the landing.

"Jimmy, just look at the state of you, you're like a bleedin' bag wash tied up ugly."

He grinned back at her and ran down the steps as fast as he could, one at a time.

*

After school Jimmy would sometimes get an invitation from his older cousin Barry who lived in Queens Cottages to go to his flat to play. Charlie Barton's younger sister Flo would serve up cocoa and biscuits for the pair of them. But his favourite after school visit was to his neighbour Mrs. Page's flat once a week to watch the 'Cisco Kid' on her new television set. He would sit self consciously more often than not on his own in Mrs. Page's parlour. She had room for a proper parlour because her two sons were married. He would follow the antics of the two overweight heroes with their excruciating Mexican accents as they made another daring rescue on the 14–inch black and white screen. The programme always ended with the Cisco Kid and his sidekick Pancho astride their horses grinning inanely at each other and saying 'Aah, Cisco', 'Aah, Pancho' and riding away in a cloud of dust. That was his signal to thank Mrs. Page for letting him watch her TV and to go home for his tea, as his mum would be home by then.

"Mum, can't we have a telly. Aunt Flo's going to get one and Steve says they're really good, and it will keep me out of mischief," and so began a long campaign of attrition to bring the goggle box into the Barton's life.

Without a television set to watch the Bartons would spend the weekday evenings in a variety of occupations. Jimmy usually played out until it got too dark, unless the weather was too awful or if none of his friends were around. Indoors he would read comics and draw, but he was prone to bouts of lethargy and boredom.

Mr Barton would usually be absorbed in the 'Daily Express' or the 'Evening News' while Jimmy's mum took on the exasperating job of keeping Jimmy occupied.

*

"You're a funny boy Jimmy. There must be something you want to do."

Then Mr. Barton joined in.

"When I was your age I wasn't even allowed indoors except for a bite of food and to sleep. Mum's place was full of kids. And adults too, wanting a bit of peace and quiet.

I was sent out every day on errands – I was always round the dispensary getting my dad's stomach medicine – and I was always hungry and scrumping off Gutteridge's the greengrocer's. We had to make our own pleasures. We didn't have all the toys and books that you've got, and we certainly had no time to be bored."

He went back to the Evening News crossword.

"Look, why don't you help me with these powder puffs, you can turn the cases inside out for me?" suggested Mrs. Barton.

Jimmy slouched half heartedly into an armchair and reached out to the box of pastel powder puff cases.

"You'd better wash your hands first Jimmy."

"Why?"

"I don't want grubby marks on them, they wouldn't thank me for that."

"Why?"

"You know bleedin' why Jimmy," Mr. Barton piped up, "Come over here and help me with this crossword if you won't help your mother."

So they did the Evening News children's crossword together and then filled in the picture crossword which was very easy unless a drawing was so ambiguous that it even stumped Mr. Barton.

"See who's at the door Jimmy." At the sound of the knock he was out of his chair and needed no more encouragement.

"It's Terry, I'm going out," he shouted back from the passage.

"Alright dear, don't make it late, I don't want to have to come out looking for you...." But he was already gone, "Well that's a relief," Mrs. Barton said as she turned out another pristine powder puff.

*

Charlie Barton mostly stayed at home in the evenings except on Fridays and weekends when he did his piano playing duties in the Packington Arms. On weeknights after lingering over dinner he would read the papers and smoke. On summer evenings he would take a chair on to the balcony and glory in the sunshine with his cigarettes and cups of tea to hand, and chat with the neighbours. Although he was a sociable man he had no special friends and certainly nobody ever came round to visit. It was as if he lived in three separate worlds which never overlapped, work life, family life, and social life in the pub. Martha Barton seemed to be quite happy with this arrangement for although she could handle social occasions if she had to, she would rather 'not be bothered with people' as she put it. Family, duty and work were more important to her.

But despite her inclination to live and let live her sense of duty had impelled her to help organise the street party in Cornwall Cottages for the Coronation of 1953, as very few others seemed willing to help out. Every block down the Street had its own Coronation Committee that raised money, bought decorations, and organised kids' parties and fancy dress competitions. Much to Mr. Barton's chagrin, his wife was in the Cornwall Cottages' vanguard, ignoring her familial duties and using her own money to top up the funds when necessary. At least that is what he suspected. She even found time to make Jimmy a spaceman's suit and helmet for the kids' fancy dress competition. She was relieved that he did not win because tongues would have wagged. But the spaceman's short trousers and long socks ensured that Jimmy did not even reach the short list (See illustration 10).

Jimmy's favourite radio programme was broadcast on Monday evenings. It was called 'Journey Into Space' and was accompanied by eerie radiophonic music that was more frightening than the impossibly dangerous situations that Captain Jet and his cheeky Cockney lieutenant Lemmy, who were lost in space, found themselves in at the end of each cliff hanging episode. He spent hours listening to radio programmes like 'Meet The Huggetts', 'Take It From Here' and 'Have a Go', and even 'The Archers' which Mrs. Barton followed avidly. They usually came on after dinner when his mum got out the ironing or settled down to some sweatshop homework. They would listen together and laugh out loud but Mr. Barton only half listened, he preferred the papers. He was not even stirred when Grace Archer died in the fire at Brookfield Farm and he thought that Ron Glumm and his affianced Eth were pathetic.

The good thing about the radio was that they could do other things while they were listening. Jimmy would mostly doodle with his Venus colouring pencil set, often on the backs of his mother's 'Excelsior' cards if she was sewing on buttons. If she was not doing homework, or mending or altering clothes, or knitting, or making rag rugs, she would do the ironing while listening to June Whitfield plead with her 'bee–luv–ed' Ron Glumm, alias Dick Bentley, to name the day.

Mrs. Barton's evening activities were all sedentary except for ironing. This not only involved standing and ironing at the old multi–purpose kitchen table suitably covered with an old doubled up scorched blanket, but it also involved going in and out to the scullery stove. While one flat iron was on the gas ring being heated Mrs. Barton would be wielding the other in the back room. She was adept at judging, with the use of a wetted finger, when the iron was cool enough to use but inevitably there were mishaps. Charred iron shapes were incised into the tabletop and holes were burned in the soft rags she used for gripping the iron. She sometimes forgot to remove them when she put the iron on the gas.

*

"It's a wonder you ain't caught the scullery alight," shouted Mr. Barton as he gingerly threw a flaming rag into the Butler sink and turned the tap on.

"It's lucky I came out here to make a cup of tea."

"Sorry dear, I was engrossed in the Glumms," Mrs. Barton said as she rushed in behind her husband, "You'll have to get me an electric iron."

"But we've only had electricity for five minutes."

"No electric iron, no shirts," she said as they returned to the back room just as Jimmy Edwards came in from the 'Frog and Nightgown' to find Ron and Eth inflagrante on the Glumms sofa.

"Yes, you're probably right Martha. You'd better see the Dawsons' man about it on Saturday."

"And what about an ironing board as well?"

"One thing at a time Martha, please," he laughed. He was only half–serious.

*

When things were quiet Mrs. Barton liked to read magazines, usually the 'Woman's Own' or the 'Woman's Weekly' and sometimes magazines about antiques, but more often she would read her favourite books. She was very selective, and often read the same book several times. She only had a small book collection of her own, mostly Dickens, Walter Scott's and other Victorian novels which she had bought years before from 'the old dears who sold bits and pieces up Essex Road'. Her favourite book was 'Pickwick Papers'

"I first read Pickwick Papers when I was a girl. I used to sit in the passage in our house in Hoxton and roar with laughter. 'She's reading again' my mum used to say. 'But it's really funny mum,' I told her but she thought it was me who was the funny one. In Hoxton a book was only as good as what you could sell it for."

Every couple of weeks usually on Saturday afternoons, Jimmy's mum would go to the lovely Carnegie library in Essex Road to borrow some historical novels or Agatha Christie's, and sometimes she would take Jimmy with her. It was a beautiful building, almost as good as the Carlton cinema in Jimmy's eyes, and he loved the highly polished timber floors and shelves and counters and the smell of books and furniture polish. He would be under strict orders to keep quiet and not to run around but he must have been a hindrance to her browsing satisfactorily. His favourite pastime was to slide on his bum surreptitiously along the polished steps that stretched along half of one of the walls of the adult library without attracting the attention of the librarian.

"You'll get me thrown out one day Jimmy," she would say as they stepped into the glorious marble entrance hall of the library and out into the real world.

Jimmy became a member of the children's library in his last year at Charlie Mutton's. One day Miss Steifle trooped the whole class up Pickering Street and across Essex Road to the library and after they were formally enrolled all the children chose books to take back with them. Jimmy was torn between finding a book he would enjoy reading and finding one that would impress everybody. To his shame he decided to take the thickest book with the most pages he could find. It happened to be Captain Marryat's 'Mr. Midshipman Easy'. But easy it was not. However he persevered over many weeks and finished it, but nobody was impressed, except Jimmy who saw it as an endurance test. At least it did not put him off reading books altogether, but nor did it wean him off comics.

Sally Barton would spend most of her evenings away from the Cottages, either with her boy friend Tommy Wilson, or with her friends from the Street or her old friends from Owen's school. But for a few years she studied short hand typing at The City of London College, and also she took up cookery classes. She had been too busy with schoolwork to find time to cook at home, and her mother was disinclined to involve her in the daily preparation of meals. But now that she was engaged to be married it seemed appropriate that she should learn how to boil an egg, as Mr. Barton put it. So once a week she would bring home something she had cooked at evening classes, and would be ribbed by Mr. Barton for it. Jimmy was particularly keen to try out his sister's culinary efforts, especially if they were what he would have called 'afters', and he fell in love with her egg custard tart. It had the most exquisite taste, liberally sprinkled with ground nutmeg as it was, and he would pester his poor sister for repeat performances, which she sometimes managed to his delight.

When Sally began serious courting the front room of the Barton flat, which doubled as her bedroom and as the occasional parlour, became the courting room as well. Tom and Sally would sit on the rexine covered 'Put–U–Up' and listen to Dean Martin and Al Martino 78s on the big new 'Ferguson' radiogram. Sometimes a few friends would come round as well. Jimmy was under instructions not to disturb his sister when Tom or her other friends were there but he thought that this was a bit unfair as she was rarely at home anyway, at least when he was up and about.

*

"Don't you go disturbing them again Jimmy," Mrs. Barton looked up from her knitting.

"But I've finished these sums Tom gave me," Jimmy whined.

Tommy had been coaching Jimmy in arithmetic, and Sally helped him with spelling and grammar because he was coming up for his eleven plus examination.

"You wait a while. They won't want you pestering them all night," said Mrs. Barton.

So Jimmy sat and sulkily doodled at the old kitchen table, when suddenly Sally opened the back room door.

"I'm making us some tea. Would you like some?" she said, and swept the teapot off the table as she turned to go out to the scullery.

"Thanks dear, make a full pot will you," said her mother.

Jimmy quickly followed her out into the passage clutching his exercise book. She turned left into the scullery and he turned right into the parlour, and Tommy Wilson checked his arithmetic. He stayed long enough for Tom to write down a new set of sums, and to cajole the promise of a game of cards from him the next time he came around. Sally came in with two cups of tea followed closely by Mrs. Barton who turfed Jimmy out on his ear.

"Thanks mum," Sally called out to the closing parlour door."

*

Jimmy would also get in the way when Sally's girl friends came round if his mum was not there to stop him. However he knew he was persona non grata when he sat on one of the 78s and broke it. Sally's friends could not have been too perturbed with her little brother because one of them gave him her schoolgirl stamp collection, and another gave him a ukulele, or at least she gave it to Sally and he used to play it.

The ukulele came in a green baize lined case and had a felt plectrum and a songbook with chords. Jimmy learned how to tune it to the little four note melody whose one line was 'All dogs have fleas', and got as far as being able to play 'Mobile' ('Where's that? Alabama!'). And the ukulele became indispensable when Jimmy and his friends formed a skiffle group, although a guitar would have been better. Johnny Winston made a tea chest base. Terry borrowed his Nan's old washboard and Jimmy got him a pair of thimbles from his mum's knick–knack box. Jimmy tuned up the ukulele. For three or four nights only, never to be repeated, they set up their skiffle band in the Cornwall Gate to entertain the homecoming inebriates from the Half Moon. They never practised but just dived straight in. The idea was to sing, strum and clatter as loudly and as quickly as they could through the classic skiffle repertoire of 'Rock Island Line', 'Lost John' and 'Don't you Rock Me Daddy–O'. They did not know all the words but that did not matter because it sounded like Lonnie Donnegan did not either. Homecoming Cottagers either passed by in complete disbelief at the noise reverberating around the Gate or stood and watched as the strumming and clatter became more demented and the voices cracked or momentarily stopped to allow breathing to recommence. Until exhausted and not knowing 'which–a–way Lost John g'wyne' they completely seized up, to a burst of applause and a shower of pennies. They thought they were on to a good thing but both they and the boozy bobs quickly got sick of skiffle, as did the rest of the country.

The Street kids woke up one day to find that Rock and Roll and teenagers were taking over the world. There had been a few inroads on 'Two Way Family Favourites', and many subversives were abandoning the BBC for Radio Luxembourg which had no inhibitions about playing the music of the new youth culture. As Jimmy's flat only had a 'British Relay' radio he could not listen to the pirate station but his ears were attuned to picking up the new music from anywhere in his environment. And from among the great anthems of the late 50s that Jimmy managed to latch on to, two stood out in his initiation into appreciating the music of his generation. One he heard by accident one evening outside the Gate of Albany Cottages. He passed a group of boys standing around a sub–teenager with a guitar. The guitarist was a distant relation of Jimmy from Albany, a second cousin, and his band had been on the Carol Levis children's talent show on television. So Jimmy felt entitled to listen despite being in alien territory, but the gathering was good–natured anyway.

"Yeh, it'll be in the shops tomorrow. It's been on Luxembourg all week." He strummed the simple sequence of chords and sang the words. The song was about a desperate young man in love with an older woman begging her to stick by him. It rose a tone higher every two lines and was punctuated at the end of each verse with the sobbing refrain,'Die-yanna!'

He stopped singing. "It's called 'Diana'. This bloke called Paul Anka sings it. He's only 16. 'Course, I'm singing it My Way. The record's a lot better than that. You should hear the saxophone on it."

Jimmy was convinced. He was completely seduced by the musical logic of what he had heard. The other stuff that his cousin played could not touch it. The sentiment of the song was lost on him but to many of his elders a song about a teenager's infatuation for an older woman was a pretty racy notion. It was this forbidden fruit aspect of much of the new music as well as its vitality that attracted the Street kids and repelled many adult Cottagers. Mrs. Barton was particularly appalled by the diction of the young singers.

"Why can't they open their mouths? Mumble, mumble, mumble, and 'Die–yanna', I ask you?"

The other song that made Jimmy shiver was called 'Why Do Fools Fall in Love', and this was performed by a singer even younger than Paul Anka was. Frankie Lymon was only 14. Indeed the band he sang with called themselves 'The Teenagers'. Jimmy had never heard this kind of exciting falsetto singing and doo–wop harmonies before, and he did not realise until years later that Frankie Lymon was black and that he was listening to the suppressed rhythms of an alienated culture that changed popular music forever. Of course 'The Teenagers' were not pioneers, but until Frankie Lymon got to number one in the charts Jimmy never knew that such subversive music existed. He had a similar awakening in the sixties when he first heard Jimmy Reed and electric Chicago Blues.

Jimmy Barton daydreamed about becoming a Rock and Roll hero but he had a whole lifetime ahead of him before he reached 14, and being 16 like Paul Anka was impossible to imagine. But to be almost as old as his sister, as Buddy Holly was, and to be still singing Rock and Roll meant that Jimmy had all the time in the world to make it. He never did. He never got around to it.

*

Friday was the best weekday. No more school and it was payday. Charlie Barton would come home whistling and with a brown paper parcel containing his oily overalls under his arm, a bag of fruit in his hand, and his wages in his inside pocket. He had a habit of buying apples, pears and bananas on Friday nights from his old schoolmate Fred Holloway who had a stall in Essex Road on the other side of Elder Walk from Morris the fishmonger. He liked to keep in with his many acquaintants. The fruit usually lasted all week. It would be tastefully laid out on the sideboard in two crystal bowls, wedding presents that had survived the Blitz. He was partial to a piece of fruit in the evening even though he had to peel the apples and often the pears as well because of his false teeth, and peanuts got under his plate. Bananas were ideal. He would give Mrs. Barton the housekeeping money, and Jimmy his pocket money, satisfied that another week's work had been rewarded and the weekend was about to begin. It would begin however with washing away the trials of the week. Friday night was bath night.

After the tea things were washed up, Mr. Barton would awkwardly manoeuvre the long tin bath out of its upright position behind the scullery door and lay it down in the space between the gas stove and the toilet partition. There was only just enough room to sidle around the bath to get to the sink. Every saucepan in the scullery would be filled with water and put to boil on the gas rings, but that was before Mrs. Barton acquired a 'Dinky Dean' gas boiler. The boiler was used for washing bed linen because Mrs. Barton did not believe that the bag wash was good enough and that sheets and pillowcases had to be boiled, perhaps she recalled the bed bugs of her childhood. But on bath nights the boiler was a Godsend. Mr. Barton would lift it on to the enamel topped table that converted into a mangle and fill it with water. When it was boiling and the gas was turned off, the Bartons had hot water on tap and the scullery would be temporarily converted into a bathroom.

The scalding water would be tempered with saucepans of cold, and softened with a shake from the blue and white ICI box of washing soda crystals – just enough to tenderise a corn without causing total dermatological breakdown. Sally would be the first to use the bath. Mr. Barton no longer had to watch out for feverish youths climbing on the roof to peer into the scullery window. Her generation had grown out of that, but a blanket would still be draped over the window on bath nights just in case.

Mrs. Barton would use the water next, followed by Mr. Barton, with liberal additions of hot water tumbled in from the 'Dinky Dean' in between each submersion. Jimmy would be the last in, for the obvious reason that no one would want to bath in the water after him. He did not mind at all. It meant that he did not have to hurry. The water would still be hot, and when topped up for the final time it would be deep enough for him to submerge himself from head to foot. He would play and thrash about and blow bubbles until his mother told him to get a move on, then he would wash his hair with the bar of 'Imperial Leather', and rinse it with a saucepan of warm water. Pink and prune skinned he would stand on the saturated towel that had served as a bathmat for all four of them and dry himself. He would put on the clothes that his mother had given him when she had first bundled him into the scullery, having just rounded him up from the Square. Eventually he would emerge into the passage.

Mr Barton, dressed in a clean white shirt, his suit trousers and his best brown Oxford shoes, would step past him to enter the steam–laden scullery. But before he could get shaved and slope off to the Packington Arms he would have to empty the bath. This was a bailing out job using a saucepan to transfer the week's murk into the sink. The final drop of water then had to be tipped out of the bath, which Mr. Barton would carefully balance on the edge of the saucepan. He would then put the bath back behind the scullery door. Now he could get to the sink for a shave, something he always did of an evening whether or not he was going out. While he was shaving Mrs. Barton would mop up the scullery and pile the dirty washing and towels into the upended bath.

"Time I was off Martha," he would say and she would kiss him goodbye.

"Me too," Jimmy would try his luck.

"No you don't young man," his mother would collar him, "You're all clean, for once. Anyway all the kids have gone in now. You can keep me company."

"Not 'Friday Night is Music Night' mum, they never sing anything decent." He was invariably right as excerpts from 'The Desert Song' would already be welling out of the radiogram.

"Mum, can I go up to Al's tomorrow and get Elvis Presley's 'All Shook Up'? Could you lend me the money?"

"Elvis, what sort of a name is that? I ask you?"

SATURDAY

Occasionally, on Saturday mornings Martha Barton had to go to work. She was the cook and chief washer–up at the canteen in the big clothing factory near the canal bridge on Shepherdess Walk. If 'CANDA' or 'C&A' as its retail outlets were known, had some urgent work to be done at the factory it would open on Saturday mornings and she would prepare teas and rolls and go round the factory floors with her trolley. Mr. Barton regularly complained about how she was being exploited by the canteen manager and how the factory workers took advantage of her.

"Your mother's gone down to that bleedin' canteen again," he said to Jimmy as he dished up a huge bowl of thick porridge for his son's breakfast.

He was an expert at making breakfasts and always made his own on most mornings, usually fried eggs, tomatoes and a couple of rashers, but on cold Saturday mornings, when Jimmy's mother was at work, he made thick sweet porridge for the two of them.

"That boss of hers, Mr. Ball, he knows she's a soft touch, gets her doing this for him and that for him since he made her the manageress. She comes home worn out."

Jimmy's mum worked hard and she liked to please and found it hard to say no. She loved to work and her sense of duty and loyalty always held up despite the regular admonitions from her family to be less obliging.

"That Mr. Ball thinks he's bleedin' Flying Officer Kite with that handle bar moustache of his. He grew it after he'd made his packet as a Sergeant cook in the RAF. He's got half a dozen canteens to run now. He must be rolling in it. And does he appreciate your mother? No! She don't even bring home a few bits and pieces. Another woman would bring home a couple of chops or a bit of steak. But no, not her. She says to me...'Oh, I did them a lovely steak and kidney pie today, and they did enjoy it. They came back for more'. But did she bring us home a bit? No, the silly woman. There she is cooking all day and then she comes home and cooks again for us. She'll never learn."

'Children's Favourites' was on the radio and Danny Kaye's 'Ugly Duckling' was rapidly followed by 'The Teddy Bear's Picnic'.

"And do you remember that night she didn't come home. I was worried sick. It was late – gone seven. I went down to the canal bridge and the factory was in total darkness. I was banging on the gates for five minutes before the watchman came out. I says, 'Is anybody working tonight?', 'No', he says, 'They all went home hour and a half ago'. So I says, 'Would you check to see if my missis is still there – she's the canteen cook?'. 'Does a nice bit of pie does your missis', he says. Don't I bleedin' know it. So he goes off to check. Ten minutes later he comes back with your mother and the washer–up. They've been stuck in the lift between the fifth and fourth floors ever since the watchman turned the power off. They've been in the dark, banging on the doors and giggling to themselves. She'd stayed behind to clear up and prepare something special for the governors' dinner next day as a favour to Ballsie. 'I almost had the police out after you',

I says, and she says they weren't worried because they knew Fred the watchman would be doing his rounds later on. I tell you that canteen is the bane of my life."

*

Most of the flats in the Cottages had 'British Relay' radios, which consisted of a loudspeaker, and a separate Bakelite dial fixed to the window frame. The dial had only four positions – Light Programme, Home Service, Third Programme and Off. Each block down the Street had been wired up for 'British Relay' and the signal needed no amplification, so the radio worked without batteries or electric power, which was ideal for a gas only household. The Cottagers paid the weekly rental at the 'British Relay' shop in Essex Road where the window was full of new relay TV sets for rent. When the Barton's were eventually electrified and Jimmy's mum and dad got around to acquiring a television, the obvious choice was a 'British Relay' set. It needed no aerial. When it arrived the electrician took away the old radio because there was one already built into the TV set, but now it required electricity to operate it – that's progress. The unfortunate thing about the relay radio was that it only gave the choice of the three standard BBC programmes, while Jimmy craved Rock and Roll music that could only be got by tuning in to Radio Luxembourg.

'Saturday Club' would start on the Light Programme and there was a chance that a few decent songs might be played in between the rubbish, but Jimmy could not listen for long because he always went to the pictures on Saturday mornings.

The Carlton cinema in Essex Road was a fabulous place with an Egyptian style white tiled frontage and with rows of sparkling bronze framed glass doors. The queue of kids would stretch along the side of the building which in stark contrast was of bare brickwork punctuated with barred toilet windows, soil pipes and pairs of exit doors in deep recesses containing suspicious stains and the occasional dried remains of an inebriate supper.

As soon as the doors were opened the queue would move along pretty quickly. Order was maintained by a couple of usherettes from the Gestapo. For the price of sixpence the children were allowed to pass through the plush foyers, no loitering allowed, and into the huge auditorium that was in uproar until the lights went down. The programme would start with a rousing rendition of the 'ABC Minors' song, which was sung to the tune of Souza's 'Blaze Away', and was accompanied by a bouncing ball moving from word to word on the screen.

"We are the boys and girls well known as,

Minors of the ABC,

And every Saturday we line up,

To see the films we like and shout aloud with glee.

We like to laugh and have a singsong,

Such a happy crowd are we–ee.

We're all pals together,

We're Minors of the ABC."

The song would build up to an enormous yelling crescendo on the last 'ABC' and then everyone would settle back to watch the first 'Looney Tunes' cartoon.

The cartoons were followed by an edifying documentary film about far away places, and by the next episode of the 'Flash Gordon' serial. Then 'Pearl and Dean' would instill the kids with an overwhelming desire for cold sugary substances and the octogenarian ice cream ladies would appear from nowhere with trays of 'Orange Maid' ice–lollies and choc–ices. The lights would come on, a hundred tip–up seats would bang and a pair of disorganised queues would instantaneously develop in the side aisles. The second half of the programme was usually a 'B' Western accompanied by airborne lolly sticks, chewing gum and sweet wrappers lit up like shooting stars in the beam of flickering light jabbing down from the projection room. The Baddies would finally bite the dust to a great cheer, and the kids would pour out from the cinema to the clatter of panic bolts and calls of recognition as squinting eyes spotted mates from school and the Street. Jimmy and Terry would part company in the Gate of Cornwall Cottages after discussing the morning's entertainment. Their critic's credentials, 'ABC Minors' badges, would be proudly displayed on their jacket lapel. Jimmy had gone home after many a session of Saturday morning pictures wondering what it all had to do with mining.

Charlie Barton would get his hair cut on Saturdays and he always took Jimmy with him. Hair cuts were a kind of ritual which began with an army style walk along Essex Road to Islington Green where the Italian barber had his shop next to the 'Shakespeare's Head'.

"Jimmy you're supposed to hold your head up, chest out and swing your arms. That's right son. We had to do a lot of square bashing during the war. It was all blanco and bull but we did well on it. I was A1 fit then, it says so in my army pay book."

So it was hup two three to Tony the barber's for short back and sides.

They would pass 'The Queen's Head', which his mum said was haunted by Sir Walter Raleigh. The pub stood opposite the old 'Clothworkers' almshouses, which were real cottages with flower gardens and roses round the door unlike the Cottages down the Street. Then they would pass Nash's, Mrs. Barton's favourite second hand jewellery shop, and then Dorietis', which was Jimmy's favourite ice cream shop. Dorietis was a shiny white enamelled café, which in summertime also sold home made ice cream out of one of it's front windows. Sometimes his dad would buy him a wafer on the way back from Tony's and he would savour that first cold lick along one edge of the thick ice cream sandwich. Then rapidly he would wizz round all four edges with his tongue, scooping out the deliciously sweet vanilla flavoured ambrosia, which was interspersed with tiny slivers of ice. Then he would squeeze the wafers together to force more ice cream out towards the edges and lick all round again. The wafer sandwich grew thinner and thinner and the wafers would start to disintegrate and take on the grubby impressions of Jimmy's eager digits. When he could squeeze out no more ice cream he would nibble at the insalubrious wafers until all he had left was a bunch of sticky fingers.

At Islington Green they would pass the Collins Music Hall. Jimmy had been taken there once by his dad. It was on this stage that he had encountered a naked lady for the first time. She was posing in an artistic and strictly static tableau. And diagonally across from the music hall on the Angel side of the Green was Tony the barber's where Mr Barton had been getting his hair cut ever since he had been de–mobbed in 1946. They would step inside and Tony would greet them as he looked up from his snipping.

Jimmy would sit and wait, fascinated by the paraphernalia of the barber's shop – photos of Mediterranean looking men with DA haircuts, rows of creams and bottles, glass cabinets full of razor blades and packets of contraceptives, singeing tapers and rubber powder puffers for red necks. Someone would be getting a shave and Tony would hone his cut–throat razor on the long leather strop hanging on the wall next to the hot towel machine. He would make deft swipes at the soap around the ears of his trusting customer.

"If he cuts his ear off, can I have it?" Jimmy's dad would comment in his best Al Reid imitation.

Tony's assistant would cut Jimmy's hair, but first he would place a short plank of wood across the arms of the barber's chair to get him to the right height. Then he would run the hand clippers up Jimmy's neck and make him shiver.

On the way home from the barber's they usually stopped at the newspaper stall outside the Half Moon to pay Wally the paper boy for the week's newspapers, and to get Jimmy's 'Beano' and 'Beezer'. While his father had a few words with Wally, Jimmy would read up on the latest instalment of 'The Bash Street Kids'. Sometimes the comics came with a free gift such as a cardboard clapper or a spinning cardboard disc, which was supposed to make a high pitched whine. The clappers were good, but they only lasted for an hour or so. They consisted of triangles of cardboard and stiff brown paper, which were glued to each other along two edges. The whole thing was folded down the middle to form a smaller triangle with the brown paper on the inside, and it was fitted with a cardboard handle. By holding the clapper high and bringing it down hard, the paper and the cardboard could be made to part company with a loud clap as the inrush of air forced the paper outwards. After half a dozen hefty claps the paper would start to split. Unfortunately for the kids but fortunately for their parents, it was a five–minute wonder. When several clappers were going at once, and in increasing competition with each other, the Cottagers could get rather exasperated with the noise.

"As if the kids don't make enough bleedin' noise without them giving away those bloody things with the comics," Wally the paperboy would remonstrate with his customers.

"Yes, but it helps keep them out of mischief Wally. And Jimmy, if you bang that thing indoors I'll stick your arse under the cold tap."

Jimmy liked to be out with his father. The occasional Saturday morning was the only time they spent alone together. At Jimmy's instigation his father would talk about the war. Jimmy found the stories of privation, separation, and destruction the most interesting episodes of his parents' life. He never tired of listening to them over and over again.

*

"I used to know a Maltese boy about your age Jimmy. It was during the Blitz. I was just out of hospital – sand fly fever they said it was – and I wasn't fit enough to go back to the gun pit in Valletta (see illustration 11). They got me out delivering rations to the gun pits around the airfield at Ta Qali and this boy used to come round with me with his donkey cart. He used to lead the old donkey and I would walk along beside him. We didn't talk much, couldn't, his English wasn't up to much and nor was my Maltese. It was a fair old whack around the outside of the airfield, along country lanes. Course, we was always hungry, no ships were getting in, and we used to eat oranges from the trees, sometimes green ones, peel and all. The planes would come over from Sicily to bomb the airfields."

"The Hurricanes and Spitfires would get up there pretty sharpish. Bloody noise! Bombs and Ack–Ack. The Stukas were the noisiest. Once we got caught out in an air raid between gun pits and they were getting bloody close. He jumped up and down and swore at Jerry, you know, a lot of Maltese jabber. We dived down at the side of the road. I had my tin hat and rifle, but the boy had nothing and I laid across him, schrapnel all over the place. Yes, he was a good kid and we got on all right. Course, when the MO said I was fit, I was back on the old 'Bofors' again. I never saw him after that, but I heard he'd got killed in an air raid. Those Maltese were all like that – brave they were. Always coming out with 'Ave Marias' and crossing themselves. I liked them a lot."

*

On Saturday mornings Jimmy's mum would leave out little piles of coins on the dining table for the milkman, the insurance men and the tallyman from Dawsons. Whoever happened to answer the door would pay the man his money. The insurance men in shiny suits had books with elastic bands round them in which they recorded the paid up weekly premiums. They all came to the Barton's door, the Pearl, the Prudential, the Liverpool Victoria and the Farringdon Reliance.

"Mum, why do you have all those different insurances?" Jimmy asked as he shut the front door after paying the man from the Pru', "There are four books here just for the Prudential."

"Well there are four of us here Jimmy," Mrs. Barton explained, "And anyway, we took over a lot of them. Look at this one – taken out in 1910 by your grandmother for dad when he was a few weeks old. A ha'penny a week. It was a funeral insurance because in those days women had lots of babies and sometimes they lost them before they got very old. Scarlet Fever and Whooping Cough, and carelessness I suppose. Look, there's another one here for me, one that my mum took out. They hardly had enough to keep body and soul together without the expense of a baby's funeral as well. So all the babies were insured. Your dad's family used the Pru' and the Farringdon, and mine used the Pearl and the Liverpool Vic', so now we've got all four knocking on the bleedin' door."

It would be a relief when the last receipt book was put back in the sideboard drawer for another week. The rest of the day would be free of callers except for the Dawsons man who was generally the last. Dawsons was a departmental store near Old Street that gave credit to customers, and Martha Barton would always take out a new loan in time for Christmas. The Dawsons man appreciated customers like Jimmy's mother because she would never miss a payment and never borrowed more than she could comfortably pay back.

Jimmy usually went with her on the twice yearly trip to Dawsons if his wardrobe needed replenishing. On these occasions they would take the 611 trolley bus down New North Road to Dawsons, which occupied the prominent triangular site between City Road and East Road right opposite the Methodist 'Leysian Mission'. Jimmy was usually rigged out with a jacket and trousers and a couple of shirts. The shop assistant would stuff the receipt and the loan vouchers into a brass tube that fitted into an overhead conveyor. When the assistant pulled a lever the carrier would shoot off noisily along the track at rattling speed, like a demented miniature roller coaster, on its way to the cashier's booth. It would shortly return with change and the endorsed receipt. Jimmy was intrigued by the goings on in the departmental store and he did not mind his trips to Dawsons, but he hated shopping otherwise. This was mainly because of the interminable conversations Martha Barton would have with the neighbours she encountered on even the shortest of shopping trips along Essex Road.

Jimmy's mother would only make dinner, as lunch was called, on Sundays. Saturdays were too busy for cooking much. The usual fare for Saturday was cheese rolls and a tin of chicken soup. However Jimmy's sister Sally would sometimes cajole her mother into sending her out for meat pies and mash. Sally was very partial to pie and mash and she would rush home to the flat with a shopping bag full of paper wrapped pies, and a jam jar full of green parsley liquor. The nearest pie shop was Williams in New North road but Manze's in Chapel Market at the Angel was the Cottagers' favourite pie shop.

Manze's had coffee shop style pews with high timber backs and timber posts lining the sawdusted aisle, and with marble topped counters and tables on iron filigree legs. The shop windows on either side of the double doors were wide open to the pavement for serving pies from one and live eels from the other. All the local street markets had pie shops, there was another Manze's in Exmouth Market, Fortune's in Hoxton Street and Cooke's near Ridley Road market and the Kingsland 'Waste'.

Jimmy's mother would get the plates out of the oven while Sally opened the steaming packets of flat brown and white mottled pies, and bags of mashed potatoes, still showing signs of the coiled shapes made by the mincer. The plates would be eagerly received, and libations of vinegar, pale green liquor, and salt and pepper made over the Saturday lunchtime offering. Mr. Barton would open the back of his upside down pie with his knife and a whirl of brown gravy would flow out over the sea of green liquor on his plate. Jimmy however would stick to cheese rolls or beans on toast.

"Not shirt lifters again Jimmy! Try some of this. Lovely! You don't know what you're missing. You ain't 'alf finicky! When I was a kid I couldn't get enough of stuff like this. Mind you, we was always hungry – at least I was. I never had a boiled egg to myself, I had to share it with one of my sisters. You could get lots of different things from food shops in those days, not just pie and mash and fish and chips. My mum used to send me out for pigs trotters or faggots and pease pudding, or even for half a sheep's head – with the eye left in to see us through the week," he would laugh at the corny old joke, "We couldn't afford to be finicky."

Jimmy would pull a disgusted face and wonder how anyone could eat the green and brown mess that was being lauded by his father.

"My dad loved his fish," Mrs. Barton would join in, "He would say to mum when she brought a cup of tea out to his stall, 'Mary, I've asked Jack to put aside a big eel for me – would you pick it up on the way back'. And it would be a whopper, wriggling in the paper. And she would clean it – a slit up the middle to scrape out the innards – her thumb in the gills, she would whack it down on the board and chop chop chop – there it would be in pieces, still wriggling, and straight into the pot to stew. Sometimes he would bring home a bream for his tea – such a beautiful looking thing. And mum would have to clean it out in the yard. She scraped the scales off with a knife and they would fly off everywhere, silver and all the colours of the rainbow in her hair and on her apron."

Jimmy was not impressed by traditional fare. He would eat cod and chips and the occasional shrimp, but as for winkles, soft cod roes, lamb stew with dumplings, beef jelly from the bottom of the dripping bowl, and stomach turning jellied eels, he would pass them all over for a slice of bread and a triangle of 'Dairylea' cheese spread any day.

When Jimmy was not being dragged around the shops with his mother on Saturday afternoons, he would play in the Square or over the other side of the Street where the bomb ruins were. Although commonly known as the 'ruins', the rubble from the bombed out houses had been cleared away years before and the open levelled site was strewn with weeds, stones and bricks, broken glass and an assortment of discarded household rubbish. The ruins were a favourite haunt of the kids from the Cottages. But they were obliged to share them with the children from the neighbouring streets, as the ruins extended across several blocks. Apparently the original houses, some with basements, had been flattened one night by a single parachute land mine, courtesy of the Luftwaffe. However the ruins were big enough for everybody and were the scene of many adventurous games of Cowboys and Indians and Cops and Robbers. There were enough bricks around for the children to construct low walls that included plenty of holes for shooting through. Roofed over with bits of timber and maybe a piece of corrugated iron, the resulting pillboxes were bravely defended by the occupants who would camp out all day with the ants and the earwigs.

In the centre of the ruins beyond Britannia Row were the remains of a street which was the only spot suitable for ball games, especially cricket, but it was difficult to run on the surrounding rough ground because of the brickbats and rubbish. Injuries were common among the children and Jimmy and his friends would often traipse home with a gashed knee or elbow caught on broken glass, wire or sharp stones. Their mothers would warn them about playing on the bomb ruins but to little effect. The chestnut paling fence that was put around them at one time was soon trodden down and met its end on Bonfire Night.

The ruins were a good place to throw stones. It was relatively safe to do this here because there were no people or windows nearby. Targets of bottles and tins would be set up and contests held between the children who became excellent shots. A favourite target was a lone steel stanchion sticking up out of the ground about six feet. It would give a satisfying clang when struck by a stone, and around its base were thousands of spent missiles, the archaeological evidence of the passing of a couple of generations of post–war kids.

The ruins could also be a source of income for enterprising children. The old furniture that was often dumped there by the Cottagers would be meticulously searched for lost coins of which there could be many tucked down behind the seats of sofas and armchairs. Every boy at some time had also gone into the fire wood business, collecting wood and furniture from the ruins and chopping it up into threepenny bundles for sale in the Gate. Some children would even set up miniature forges on the ruins. They would lay small fires in brickbat grates and use them to melt the discarded printer's type they found outside a letterpress firm in Colebrook Row. A little heat under a tin lid crucible would turn the long thin slivers of metal, with their individual letter clearly embossed at the end, into a flow of quicksilver. Using sticks as handles or makeshift tongs, the hot metal would be poured into chalk moulds that had been inexpertly carved with a penknife to form simple crosses, medallions and paperweights. Unfortunately there was not much call for these wares among the Cottagers and the children themselves were too impoverished to support the trade for long.

Jimmy and his friends would spend hours over the bomb ruins, oblivious to the passing of time, relying on the clocks in their stomachs to give them some idea of when to go home. Sometimes a faint but recognisable voice calling out the name of one or other of the children, would float over from the Cottages and across to the ruins. If the call went unheeded an exasperated mother might appear at the edge of the ruins.

"Jimmy! I've been calling you for ages. Can't you hear me?"

"No mum."

"Your tea's getting stone cold. Just look at the state of you – and those are your best shoes. I don't know why I bother! Come over here and get in for your tea."

"Can I come out again after?"

"We'll see," Jimmy's mother would grab his arm and march him across the Street, into the Gate and up the stairs.

"See you later Tel," Jimmy would call out to his friend who had followed a safe distance behind.

Charlie Barton would have a smoked haddock for his Saturday tea, fried in the frying pan. Jimmy would have egg and chips but he was not averse to accepting a well–seasoned choice piece of fish from the end of his father's fork. The food on his father's plate always tasted better than his own especially the roast potatoes, and his pork chops were always more succulent. Mr. Barton was an expert at wielding the salt, pepper and mustard pots, and the juices from the frying pan and the baking tray.

Around teatime on Saturday the Square would resound with the cry of 'Star, News a' Standard.... classifi–ed'. The old newsboy would stand in the Gate and announce his arrival with a cry made almost unintelligible by his lack of teeth. All around the balconies of Cornwall Cottages, doors would open and people would stream down the stairs. They wanted the classified editions of the London evening papers not just to read about the fortunes of the Arsenal but more importantly to check their football pools coupon. Jimmy's mother did the pools, but she used to check them on Sunday against the table in the 'News of The World'. So Saturday teatime in the Barton household would remain undisturbed by the arrival of the football results.

After tea Charlie Barton would get ready to go to the pub. Jimmy's mother did not go with him because she did not like the smoke and the noise and having to talk to a lot of people she would rather not have to. But also her husband would be busy playing the piano for the other customers and would have little time to spend with her. He played the piano in the Packington Arms on Friday, Saturday and Sunday nights, and also on Sunday mornings. Jimmy's mother would stay at home and listen to the radio and knit, or read or do some piece work for the local sweatshops. Jimmy would usually keep his mother company on Saturday evenings when it got too dark to play outside. She liked to listen to the Saturday night play.

Jimmy's father would get washed and shaved and put on his best jacket and trousers. He had usually spent a couple of hours in bed on Saturday afternoon to put himself in good form for the evening's exertions. So after a kip and a fine smoked haddock he would be looking forward to his night at the ivories.

*

"I'll be off now Martha," he announced as he gathered up his wallet, cigarettes and lighter, and checked that he had his pocket notebook which was full of the titles of the songs he played, no music or lyrics, it was just an aide–memoire. He combed his once blonde hair, darkened through years of using 'Brylcream', or margarine when it was necessary, and kissed his wife goodbye.

"I won't be late tonight, usual chucking out time."

"'Bye love, enjoy yourself," Jimmy's mother saw him off and Jimmy watched him walk smartly around the balcony to the other side of the Square and down the open stairs to the Gate.

"I think your dad misses his brother more than he admits," she said to Jimmy as he came indoors, "They played in all the pubs around here at one time or another. The 'Ram and Teasle', the 'Hanbury', the 'Clothworkers'. They loved it, your dad on the Joanna and Sid on the violin. They never got much money for it, but they did enjoy it. It's a shame your Uncle Sid died so young."

Jimmy's Uncle Sid had lived with his two sisters, Rose and Rene, in the dark first floor flat in Cornwall Cottages overlooking the Airey between Cornwall and Edinburgh. The three of them had never left the family home and in middle age they still polished and cleaned the furniture left by Jimmy's grandmother. Sid, who had been ten years older than Jimmy's father, was only 56 when he died and the two spinster sisters still carried on polishing as well as doing the cleaning at 'Holy Joe's', the Roman Catholic church in Colebrook Row. They had converted late in life, and Charlie Barton used to joke about his sisters having 'Holy Water'.

"Course, it was Sid who got your dad playing in the first place. When they all lived at number 56 Sid used to work for 'Payton's', the music shop in Camden Passage, and at weekends he used to borrow musical instruments and bring them home. Mandolins, mouth organs, violins – they tried them all. They even had a harmonium at one time. Eventually Sid bought a piano. I don't know how they found room for it with eight of them in a flat no bigger than this one. Dad could pick up a tune as quickly as anything and in any key – they get some awful singers in that pub, right boozy bobs, but your dad manages to accompany them, even if he doesn't know the song he soon gets the hang of it. Mind you, he says they get some who can sing really well and that makes all the difference."

Jimmy's dad had an ear for music. He had no training but could pick out tunes, almost entirely on the black notes, and with a simple left hand vamping style, he could play from a repertoire of hundreds of songs from 'Autumn Leaves' to 'Roll Out The Barrel'. He practised at home and tried out the new songs he took a fancy to that he had heard on the radio, and sometimes Jimmy's mother sang along in the scullery. The black upright piano in the front room was his pride and joy.

"Look at that piano over there, your father polishes it 'til it shines like snot on a sweep's arse. It's the bane of my life. Still I can't complain, it was his piano playing that attracted me to him in the first place. I met him at a party up near Canonbury Square and of course he was playing the piano. He was in great demand at parties in those days. There were few gramophones around then but plenty of pianos. And what with his blonde hair and blue eyes I couldn't say no could I?"

"When I left Marks and Spencer's to get married and have Sally they gave me twenty pounds for a leaving present – it was a lot of money then. I talked it over with your dad and we spent it on a second hand piano. There were plenty of other things we needed, what with the new baby arriving, but I could see how much it meant to him. So I got married to your dad and the piano at the same time."

*

Jimmy was fascinated by the piano and marvelled at the intricate workings that were exposed when his father occasionally took off the front panels to dust it or when he called in the blind piano tuner, who also played in pubs. It was jet black with a mother of pearl motif tastefully inlaid in the front panel and with the inscription 'Rudolph Schumann – Berlin' on the underside of the lid to the keyboard. Jimmy was allowed to tinkle on it and he had taught himself to play the 'Dam Busters' March' and 'The Breeze and I' using one finger. Even if he had tried, Jimmy's father could not have taught his son how to do something that he himself only did by instinct, and Jimmy never progressed any further.

His sister Sally however could pick out tunes, and she would play the songs she had sung at school such as 'The Merry Pipes of Pan' and 'Linden Lea' in a style completely different to her father's. When electricity arrived in the Barton household she persuaded her father to buy a radiogram. It was as big as a sideboard and on Sunday mornings the flat would be filled with music from the popular piano concertos of Grieg, Rachmaninov and Tchaikovsky. After the record had finished Charlie Barton would pick out the romantic melodies on his piano in his own untutored way. Although he could appreciate the genius of Tchaikovsky and the skill of Eileen Joyce, he really felt more at ease with Semprini, Liberace and Charlie Kunz.

On Saturday evenings in summertime it would be light enough to play in the Square or on the ruins, but on dark winter evenings Jimmy would sit with his mother and listen to the radio or read comics. All the children in the Cottages read comics, not just the 'Beano' and 'Dandy' but also adventure comics full of cowboys and soldiers, horror, mystery and detectives. Jimmy had a small stock of comics. The British ones were mostly in black and white, except for the front page, and consisted of such titles as 'Young Marvelman' and 'Tales of The Unknown'. He also had a collection of 'Classics' comics in full colour that depicted, in lurid drawings and unforgivable language, the great stories from English literature such as 'The Time Machine' and 'Moby Dick'. Jimmy would buy a different 'Classic' every week. But the most sought after comics were the scarce American full colour comics about Superman, Batman and Walt Disney cartoon characters.

*

"Mum, I'm going down to Terry's to swap comics," Jimmy announced as he finished reading his most recent acquisition.

"Well don't be too long and don't get cold."

Jimmy walked along the balcony to the stairs and down one flight to the second floor with a thick bundle of comics under his arm. Terry lived with his grandmother in the flat directly above Jimmy's two maiden aunts, and overlooking the dingy Airey between Cornwall and Edinburgh Cottages. Terry answered the door and straightway brought his comics out into the narrow passage leading into the flat.

"Nan, I'm swapping comics with Jimmy," He called out.

Despite the cold night air the two boys sat in the passage with the front door open and presented their comics to each other in turn.

"I've read this one – ain't read that – read this...." Terry went through Jimmy's comics, "There's nine here I haven't read Jim."

Jimmy found an equivalent number of Terry's comics that he did not mind swapping. Terry was fortunate in having an aunt who was married to an American serviceman and he sometimes procured from the PX store at his airbase the coveted full colour Superman comics for Terry. The usual arrangement for swapping comics was one for one, but American ones counted for two ordinary comics and dog–eared ones counted for half. After reaching an amicable agreement, the exchange of comics was made and Jimmy and Terry placed their new acquisitions upside down at the bottom of their piles.

"Nan, I'm going down to swap comics with Johnny Winston," Terry called out as he shut the front door and stepped out behind Jimmy.

They walked along the balcony to the stairs and down two flights to the Square and so to Johnny's door. It was rumoured that John Winston had a secret hoard, but whenever he deigned to swap comics at all he only ever brought out a modest stack for perusal by the other boys.

"Do you reckon Johnny will swap comics tonight Tel?"

"He might," Terry confidently replied, "I called for him a couple of weeks ago and I got some real good'ns from him."

"Do you reckon he's got plenty stashed away then?"

"Sure, he's prob'ly got 'undreds stuffed under his bed, but I bet he won't swap any of them with us."

Johnny answered the door.

"D'ya fancy swapping comics John?" Jimmy asked.

"Depends," said Johnny, "Let's see what you've got."

Johnny thumbed through Terry's comics and then Jimmy's.

"Alright," he said, "Wait here a minute," and he disappeared inside the flat again, shutting the door behind him.

"I bet he's sorting out all his worse ones," said Jimmy after they had been waiting a few minutes.

Before Terry could comment, Johnny was back outside with a tantalising selection. The three boys settled down on the cold concrete paving outside Johnny's door, and cast their expert eyes over each other's offerings in the dim light coming from the distant lamp standard in the middle of the Square and from Johnny's front room window.

"I've never seen these ones before John, where d'ya get 'em from?" Jimmy asked, "I haven't read any of 'em."

Johnny Winston just grinned back at the other two as he sorted out one or two comics for swapping from their collections.

"Is that all you want?" asked Jimmy.

"Yeah, I've read the rest," Johnny replied.

Terry and Jimmy spent five difficult minutes choosing which of Johnny's pristine comics they would take. Johnny refused the offer of accompanying the other two on their comic swapping tour, which they intended to extend to Queens Cottages and across the Street to Quinn Buildings, and he withdrew into his flat clutching the objects of their desire.

"He only swapped one with me," Jimmy complained, "He just brought that lot out to show off, I bet."

The rest of the comic swapping excursion was more successful, and at one time involved four boys traipsing comics around the gloomy internal staircases of Quinn Buildings, and forming queues to do business with each new willing trading partner who was knocked up. With half a stack of new acquisitions to read, Jimmy and Terry agreed to swap them with each other later in the week and headed for home. But before leaving Quinn Buildings they bounced on their bums down the narrow internal flights of badly worn stone steps with their comics on their lap. Apart from comics and 'Prims', a sweet shop converted from the front room of one of the flats, the only other attraction of Quinn Buildings for the kids from the Cottages was their dangerously worn down, slide–like staircases. Cold, but well satisfied with the evening's transactions, the boys went home to warm up their bruised buttocks and to get some serious reading done.

The pubs turned out late on Saturday nights. Jimmy and his mother could hear groups of merry Cottagers making their farewells down in the Gate.

"G'night Fred, 'night Lil!"

"G'night Rose."

A full–blooded chorus of 'We'll Meet Again' welled up from below followed by shrieks of laughter.

"That'll be that lot from the Half Moon I suppose," said Jimmy's mother, "Your dad won't be long now."

They heard Charlie Barton's steady footsteps on the balcony, followed by the sound of the key in the door and the little 'whoop', or maybe it was a whistle, that he made as he came into the passage. He brought an intoxicating mixture of smells into the back room, fresh cold air, brown and mild, and cigarette smoke.

"Nice time dear?" Jimmy's mother asked.

"Not bad," he said as he walked over to the fireplace and unloaded his smoking gear on to the mantle shelf, "Quite a crowd tonight – and do you remember me telling you about Lou, that Italian bloke? – He turned up with his accordion and brought a crowd in with him and a couple of them were very good singers. Course, that bleedin' Arthur insisted on singing as usual, a bit the worse for wear and his upper set missing."

"Did anyone go round with the box dad?" Jimmy asked.

"Yeah Jimmy, not a bad night. George went round. He went in the public bar an' all – if that bleedin' Arthur does it he gets no further than his cronies by the door."

Jimmy's father pulled out from his jacket pocket a handful of coins, ha'pennies, pennies, thrupenny bits, tanners, shillings and some two bob bits and a half crown. He piled them on to the table and Jimmy sorted them out and counted them. Jimmy always stayed up on Saturday nights to count his father's piano playing collection money, and for his fee his father let him keep all the coppers older than he was, that is to say those with the head of King Edward or the old Queen on them.

"One pound, three and nine dad, and eleven pence for me."

"Keeps me in beer," Jimmy's dad smiled back as he added the coins to the others on the mantle shelf.

The governor of the Packington Arms also paid him for his piano playing; as there was no doubt that Charlie Barton made a big difference to the popularity of the pub at weekends.

"Off to bed now Jimmy," his mother said, "We'll be along soon – when Sally gets in."

Jimmy settled into his 'Utility' bed in the room he shared with his parents and read one more comic.

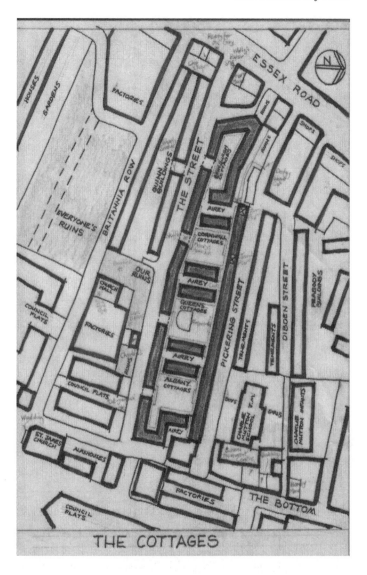

1. The Cottages – street plan

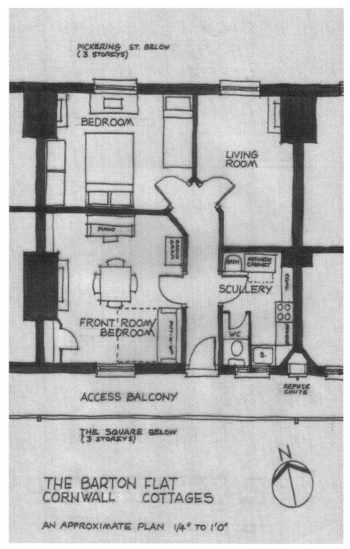

2. The Barton Flat – an approximate plan

3. Jimmy and Sally Barton, 1948

4. The access balconies of Cornwall Cottages
5. The Square, Cornwall Cottages

6. Queens Cottages from Cornwall Cottages
7. Washing lines, Cornwall Cottages

8. The Airey Between Cornwall and Queens
9. Jumble sale, for 1953 Coronation party fund

10. Fancy dress competition, 1953 Coronation
11. Charlie Barton's gun pit, Valletta

SUNDAY MORNING BLUES

On Sunday morning wet or fine
The house is steeped in gloom.
The saner members of the clan
Are chased from room to room.

Dad cowers at the piano
Pretending he's not there,
For mum is in the scullery –
She's tearing out her hair!

Jim turns on 'Family Favourites',
Then lumbers out of sight.
He's later found beneath his bed
And trembling with fright.

He'd like to make his getaway
But cannot find his shirt.
"You Charles, come out of there," mum shouts
"You're treading in the dirt."

"Aunt Flo has had her dinner.
Yes she's had it on since nine –
No thank you Mrs. Page,
I'll get along without your line."

"I think I'd better go May,
It's getting rather late."
"Go on, run off and leave me –
God this place is in a state."

Wise Sally's keeping quiet
Behind the Sunday paper.
"I'm going down the pub," said Charles,
"Cor blimey, what a caper."

"I've burnt the rhubarb tart," cried mum,
"SOD, SHIT and POOP POOP POOP!!!"
Charles ran all round the balcony
Without a second look.

Poor Jimmy's made the door at last
"Hey mum, the chute's alight."
Yelled mum, "That silly fool next door
Has stuffed it up all right."

"That Maureen's putting washing out,
Now I can't brush the mats –
And there's that funny smell again,
It must be Smithy's cat."

"Why don't you move away mum,"
Said Jimmy with a grin.
"Your father says he likes it here –
You out, or coming in?"

"You're like a walking bag wash,
Lift your feet up off the floor.
Is that Barry? – He's been up since six
And banging on the door."

"Aunt Martha, you know 'old thingy',
Well I saw him on the telly."
"Shut the door – I've got no custard
And I haven't made the jelly."

"Your father home already?"
"Hello May" – "Don't come in here!"
"Go in the front room dad," said Sal,
"I'll give you the all–clear."

At last there's peace and quiet,
A solemn stillness reigns
Till mum can't find her saccharines,
Then off we go again.

A contemporary verse by Sylvia Wilson.

SUNDAY

Sundays in the Cottages revolved around dinner – it's preparation, it's consumption and it's digestion. It was the high point of the week. The unmistakable smell of roasting meat and boiling brassicas would pervade every balcony and flight of stairs by noon. The Cottage wives would have been slaving in their sculleries all morning and the culmination of their labour was well on the way by the time Billy Cotton was calling out 'Wakey! Wake–ay' over hundreds of Cottage relay radios.

Jimmy's household was not exempt from the weekly ritual of the Sunday dinner. His mother would begin her preparations early and spend the morning cooking and cleaning. The ferocious intensity with which she carried out her onerous responsibilities was in stark contrast to the air of Sunday dissipation surrounding the other members of the family. Jimmy would spend as long as he could in bed reading his comics. His father would potter around the flat getting ready for his lunchtime piano playing session at the Packington Arms, and his sister Sally would play a few 78s on the radiogram, a Judy Garland or a Billy Eckstein song, or would tinker on the piano. In summer she was probably well out of it, playing tennis over Highbury Fields with her friends from Dame Alice Owen's.

It was somehow unnatural for any of the family to lend a hand, or rather to interfere, for the rites surrounding Sunday dinner had the inviolability of ancient tradition, accepted by all.

The scullery in Jimmy's flat was minuscule, as were all of the sculleries in Cornwall Cottages, apart from those on the ground floor where the flats had been modernised. It measured not much more than eight feet by ten feet, and one corner of this inadequate space was taken up by the WC, which was separated from the rest of the scullery by a close–boarded wooden partition. Along the walls of the resulting L shaped room were ranged all the conveniences necessary for modern Cottage life (See illustration 2).

Just behind the door to the scullery at one end of the L stood a long galvanised bath, leaning against the wall up–ended and resting on one of its handles. In this position it served as the dirty laundry receptacle, but its shape ensured that one garment too many would cause the lot to slide on to the floor, especially if the door was banged against it. Standing tall and proud next to the bath was the kitchen cabinet. It was a genuine piece of furniture in polished hard wood veneer with doors top and bottom containing decorated panes of glass in fretwork openings. The central flap could be pulled down to create a cantilevered working surface of white enamelled steel. The bottom of the cabinet was the Cottage larder and the top contained the crockery and glassware.

Next to the cabinet and pushed tight against the corner was a galvanised coal box. It had a lift up top and a sliding door at the bottom in the middle of one long face, from which the coal bucket could be filled. There was always coal dust on the lino. The box could take a couple of hundred weight. 'Lockey' the coal merchant, whose yard was behind the

Essex Road library, delivered twice a week. From the lorry parked in the Street the coalman would skillfully snatch each long sack on to his back and without a pause he would climb the three flights of stairs and hobnail his way around the balcony to Jimmy's flat. He would shoot the coal into the box with an almighty roar and a cloud of dust.

Mrs. Barton had a continuous battle with dust and she rejoiced when the black cast iron range in the front room was finally replaced with a golden gas fire. The coal box ended up with the range on the bomb ruins. Although she did not miss having to blacklead the range, rake out the cinders, lay the fire in the grate and pumice the hearthstone, Mrs. Barton did miss the fireglow and the ready hot water in the big old kettle. And Jimmy missed the ritual of toast making on cold evenings and his dad showing him how to burst bloater egg sacks on the hot fireguards.

Next to the coal box in the scullery, on its four stumpy legs was the blue and grey mottled gas stove upon which Sunday's culinary wonders would be created. Then came the mangle. This was a useful space saving device because when the mangle was not being used for de–watering the washing, it could be flipped over to create a small enamel topped table with the mangle hanging underneath. At the end of the L shaped scullery, beneath the very narrow, double–hung sash window was a shallow stoneware sink astride dwarf brick walls leaving space for a bucket in between. To one side of the sink on the floor next to the mangle was a 'Dinky Dean' gas boiler used for washing the whites and for heating up the bath water on bath night. Above it was a home made wooden draining board with one corner chamfered off to fit the angled corner of the scullery where the refuse chute was situated. At one time there had been an internal hopper opening into the chute directly opposite a similar one in the scullery next door and neighbourly conversations or blazing rows could be held across the narrow and smelly void. These openings

J.J. Rawlings

had been bricked up to discourage vermin getting into the sculleries, and communal hoppers had been installed on the external wall of the chute between the adjacent scullery windows, and were accessible only from the balconies. The chutes had been designed with dust and ashes in mind and were now too narrow for the increasing amount of packaging that was being stuffed into them. Blockages and fires in the chutes were so common that Mrs. Barton got into the habit of wrapping her rubbish in newspaper and carrying it downstairs to the refuse bins.

It was within the narrow confines of the scullery that Jimmy's mother would spend much of Sunday morning. Her first task would be to ensure that all those who were going to wash had taken their turn at the Butler sink. Jimmy was always the last to be turfed out. He was a late developer when it came to self–motivated cleansing, and he required encouragement from his mum. Standing at the sink in his vest and pants Jimmy would revolve his lathered hands slowly around his cheeks like the lady in the 'Camay' soap advertisements at the pictures. He would recall how as a small child he used to stand in the same sink and peer over the net curtains strung across the lower of the window sashes while his mother washed him down.

*

"Come on Jimmy! I've got to get the potatoes on. And look at your neck – it's ground in – and your father will be in here soon wanting to shave. Come on, I've not got all day!" Jimmy's mother said without looking up from the kitchen cabinet where she was cutting neat crosses in the ends of brussel sprouts and tossing them into the colander. In desperation she seized the face flannel lying expectantly on the draining board and delivered the finishing touches to Jimmy's half washed face and neck. She checked his arms for tell–tale tide marks and then banished him from the scullery.

After dressing himself in the bedroom Jimmy joined the other banished members of the family in the front room. Jimmy's sister was keeping out of harm's way behind the 'News of The World' and his father was polishing up his rendition of 'Red Roses For a Blue Lady' on the piano.

"What's it like out there Jimmy?" his father asked as he stroked his unshaven chin, "I'll have to go soon."

Charlie Barton was dressed in his shirtsleeves and his braces were dangling from the waistband of the trousers of his best suit. On his feet he wore a highly polished pair of brown Oxford shoes and waiting on the table were his white collar, with it's front and back studs, and his gold cuff links.

"Mum's peeling the potatoes," Jimmy replied, "It's not safe yet."

Jimmy's father had been harried from room to room by his wife for most of the morning as she dusted, swept floors, made beds, ironed Sunday clothes, prepared the Sunday joint and desperately admonished people not to tread in the dirt. He had finally found a haven in the front room where in comparative peace he had polished his shoes, the piano and it's keys, and all the bits of brass he could find. Polishing was the only household task he undertook. It gave him a lot of pleasure on Sunday mornings to see the piano in spotless condition. But he took his greatest pride in shining up the two tall brass shell cases which he had brought home from the war and which stood like altar pieces on the mantel shelf, each containing an assortment of shirt buttons, pins and elastic bands. Jimmy was intrigued by these mementoes of his father's wartime trade.

"They held the shells from our Bofors ack–ack gun – it's short for anti–aircraft Jimmy. The guns came from Sweden, light ack–ack they were, only 40mm. The Germans had them and all," Jimmy's father explained as he showed him the small indentation in the heavy base of the shell case where the firing pin had detonated the explosives inside.

"Each gun pit had three men just to keep the gun fed with clips of these shells – four to a clip, and they were bleedin' heavy too. Me and my mate were on the gun sights. We would turn the handles and the gun would swing around and up and down until we got a plane in our sights. Only when we both called out 'On' would the Sergeant press down the pedal and boom, boom, boom, boom – the flak would go up and these things would clatter out, red hot, all around the gun. We would follow the plane until the order came to switch to another target. Our gun was in Valletta's Barracca Gardens near the entrance to the Grand Harbour. The barrage we put up was deafening. They were after the ships in the harbour, trying to starve us out but sometimes Jerry would come straight for us, a Stuka or a 109. I could see the bleedin' pilot's face in my gun sight. When the plane was too close to be in range we were ordered to take cover behind the sandbags, but that would have been little use if we'd got a direct hit. Those pilots were brave men, what with all the stuff we were throwing up at them. Plenty ended up in the sea and the harbour." (See illustration 11.)

Jimmy's mother came into the front room and announced, broom in hand, that it would be the next room to be blitzed. Jimmy's sister decided that it was time to meet up with her friends.

"I'll be back for dinner mum," she promised as she stepped over the neat pile of dust in the middle of the passage floor on her way to the front door.

"I'll have a shave now Martha."

"Mind the dirt out there, and leave the gases alone – I've got the dinner on," she warned as her husband made his getaway to the scullery.

He had a habit of turning out unattended gas rings and ovens as an economy measure even if there was an assortment of saucepans and baking trays covering the stove and every shelf in the oven.

"And don't you get under my feet either Jimmy. God this place is in a state! And who's that banging on the door?"

"I'll get it mum," said Jimmy as he backed into the passage.

"And mind the dirt!"

"OK mum."

Sunday morning was a popular time for visiting relatives. Jimmy's mum and dad had numerous brothers and sisters and Jimmy had a variety of cousins. Mrs. Barton said that her nieces and nephews were turned out of the house especially on Sunday mornings and sent round to pester her so that their mothers could get on with their housework.

"It's Leslie and Chrissie mum," said Jimmy as he brought his Aunt Violet's two younger girls into the front room. Jimmy was very shy in the presence of his girl cousins and he kept up an embarrassed silence during their visit. They mostly giggled.

"Hello Aunt Martha," they said.

"Are your mum and dad alright?" Jimmy's mother asked as she put her broom aside and wiped her hands on her apron.

"Fine."

"That's good. And Jacky and the baby, and Aunt Alice and Uncle Bert?"

"They'll all be round home for dinner today so mum's pretty busy. Dad said to tell Uncle Charlie that he'll see him in the pub later on."

"That'll be nice," said Jimmy's mother who knew that her brother–in–law would be after a small loan.

She did not mind because she knew her younger sister had difficulty making ends meet with three children under twelve to bring up back in Hoxton. Jimmy's cousins stayed for a cup of tea and shortly afterwards left with the customary shilling apiece by which time his father had completed his shave, and with his hair brushed and collar and tie in place he also said goodbye.

"I'll be off now Martha," he said as he poked his head around the door of the scullery where she was peeling two huge Bramleys for the apple pie.

"That's right go off and leave me," she joked.

"You know you like to have the place to yourself on Sunday mornings," he reassured her.

"Sure, you enjoy yourself dear."

"I can't let them down, can I?"

"Jimmy will keep me company."

He closed the front door certain that on his return he would find the atmosphere more relaxed. Before walking round to the Packington Arms he would look in on his two sisters with the Holy Water and he would probably leave them with a few shillings as well.

*

Mrs. Barton would return to her scullery and begin her work with a mighty war cry of "'Right!' she cried, waving her wooden leg, and falling arse over head", which may have had something to do with Sarah Bernhardt. Left on his own in the front room Jimmy would turn on the radio and listen to 'Family Favourites' in the hope of hearing something remotely up to date. After reading out long lists of good wishes and birthday greetings from mums, dads, aunts, wives, cousins and sisters to various conscripts serving with the British Army on the Rhine in places only referred to by a BFPO number, June Metcalf would play excruciating records. The songs were about 'laying down your arms and surrendering to mine', or about pink and blue tooth brushes falling in love with each other, or even about twin babies with twenty tiny fingers and toes and dimples in unmentionable places. Eventually Jimmy's patience might be rewarded by Frankie Lane facing the barren wastes without a trace of water, or if he was really lucky somebody might request a record by the Everly Brothers.

If the music got too dreadful he would see how things stood in the scullery. Jimmy liked to watch his mother cooking. Without ever doing the jobs himself he knew how to peel potatoes, prepare brussels and roll out pastry, and how to cut off the excess pastry hanging over the apple pie dish with one hand while deftly twirling the dish with the other. He knew how to do these things merely from watching his mother on innumerable Sundays.

*

"Mum have you got any pastry left over?" he asked as she made thumb prints around the edge of the apple pie and placed some pastry petals on top to finish it off.

"You can have these little bits, but don't go making a mess and hurry up because I've got to get this washing up done."

Jimmy made a couple of rather grubby jam tarts. His mum placed them on a spare bit of shelving in the oven where they joined the apple pie, a tray of plain and coconut cookies, a dish with a nicely risen Yorkshire pudding, and the big tin containing sizzling belly of pork surrounded by roasting potatoes and an occasional parsnip. Then he went back in the front room to listen to 'Life With The Lyons' and 'Educating Archie', or it might have been 'Ray's a Laugh' and 'The Clitheroe Kid'. Mrs. Barton came in to lay the table that had pullout leaves to make it longer.

"Here Jimmy, put out the knives and forks for me. Where's your father, he's cutting it fine?"

Mr. Barton arrived with a bottle of cream soda in his hand and a 'Mackeson' in his pocket.

"I'm back Martha! Do you want your stout now or later on?" he called out.

"You can pour it now dear, I'll drink it out here."

He took the bottle of Mackeson out to the scullery and came back with half a glass of milk into which he poured some cream soda for Jimmy.

"Here Jimmy. This'll stop your farting in church. It's chaos out there. Your mother's running about like a blue arsed fly – pots and steam all over the place."

Martha Barton arranged the roasted potatoes on the heated plates and put them back in the oven. She carved the meat and thickened up the gravy in the baking tin with 'Bisto', and placed the slices of pork on to the plates, with plenty of fat and crackling for Mr. Barton and only lean for Jimmy. Finally she quartered and shared out the Yorkshire pudding and spooned out the brussel sprouts. Meanwhile Sally had returned and was now sitting expectantly with her brother and her father in the front room at the extended table with it's spotless table cloth.

The dinner arrived, the pubs were shut, and the Square was deserted. Jimmy's mother finally took off her apron and sat down. She took a long draught of 'Mackeson'.

"Well, that's another job jobbed!" she exclaimed. Not quite however, the apple pie had yet to be served up and the custard had to be made.

*

Charlie Barton would get up at 6.00 o'clock after his Sunday afternoon nap. The washing up would have been done and the scullery, which earlier had looked like the Augian Stables, would be back to normal and now freely accessible. Sometimes Jimmy's mother joined his father in the Sunday siesta. It was quite a common thing among the Cottagers to take to their beds after their bout of Sunday over–indulgence, especially if they could pack their kids off to Sunday school and have the flat to themselves.

Sunday teatime was quite relaxed. They would have bread and butter with a cold meat salad or perhaps a plate of winkles washed down with plenty of cups of tea. Semprini's soothing voice would float down from the radio's loudspeaker, which was fixed to the wall next to the gas meter above the 'Put–U–Up'. 'Old ones, young ones.... Loved ones, neglected ones', in between the popular songs and classics he played on his Steinway, he would smooth talk the Sunday teatime audience of 'Semprini Serenade'. Or the Mike Sammes Singers would 'Sing Something Simple as cares go by'. It was as if the BBC knew that hundreds of Cottagers were now relaxing after the rigours of Sunday and required undemanding listening from their radios. Tea was usually rounded off with tinned peaches and evaporated milk. Jimmy's father would disappear once more to get washed and changed for the last piano playing session of the weekend.

If her daughter was going out Mrs. Barton might suggest a visit to the cinema and she and Jimmy would go off together, usually to the small independent flea pit in New North Road called the 'Victoria'. There were many cinemas in the area but most of them were owned by the two big chains, ABC and Gaumont, and each had the same programme of films in all of its cinemas. There was therefore a limited choice and Jimmy's mother was also restricted to going to an all 'U' programme. So she would often resort to the independent cinemas which astutely catered for parents and children when the two major distributors were showing 'A's and 'X's. However she was particular about which independent she went to.

The 'Rex' at Islington Green was rather insalubrious and was notorious as a suspected haunt of Christie the mass murderer, and the 'Empire' at the Angel was a little too far

125

away. The circle at the 'Victoria' however, was close by and reasonably clean, and Jimmy and his mother would settle down for a double bill of Dean Martin and Jerry Lewis films and a couple of ice creams and a bag of 'Butterkist'. Down below in the pit the cinema staff would try to keep order among the kids and sometimes the more unruly ones would be noisily bounced out of the emergency exits. These incidents inside the cinema did not detract from those on the screen but seemed to complement them, as did the frequent demands for quiet and the spontaneous exchange of condemnations of the 'kids of today' that would break out among the more respectable audience in the circle.

Jimmy and his mum would come home to a dark and empty flat. The key was hung on a nail on the inside of the jamb of the scullery window. She would lift the sash and retrieve it and he would wait on the balcony until his mother had switched on the lights. It was not so much that he was afraid of the dark but more that he found his own home uncomfortably alien when it was dark and nobody was at home. It had felt even stranger before they had electricity and he had to wait for his mother to light the gas mantle in the front room. He would hear her inside fumbling with the matches and muttering when the thing would not light first time. She would reassure him if the gas had run out and she had to find a shilling in her purse and in the dark, climb on a chair to put it in the gas meter. The gas would light with a pop and the gauze of the mantle would give off a yellow glow. A gentle pull on the chain hanging from the lever of the gas cock would increase the flow of gas and the front room would reassuringly come to life again. She would put the kettle on for a pot of tea and soon the pubs would be turning out and his father would be home with another pocketful of coins to be counted.

THE SUMMER HOLIDAYS

At the end of July all scholarly obligations would cease at Charlie Mutton Junior Mixed School. The long days and mild weather of the summer term had already allowed Jimmy and his friends to play out very late in the Square and on the bomb ruins. But now they had 45 days of the school holidays as well, an eternity to spend doing the things they liked best. They would play seemingly endless games of 'King–he', 'Queen–he', 'Knocking–down Sticks' and 'Tin–Tan Tommy' in the Square, or they would play 'Cowboys and Indians' and 'Cops and Robbers' over the ruins. Cricket was sometimes attempted in the Square even though balls and windows did not mix and nobody had a proper bat. Roller–skating and bike riding were almost as popular but not everyone had access to skates and bikes. And on hot still days they would play marbles, hopscotch, cobs or 'hang–man' in huddles dotted around the Square.

The concrete paving would quickly become festooned with chalked hopscotch courts each with 'London' written at the top end, and with 'Wurlies' drawn in the corners of many of the numbered squares. A 'Wurlie' was a cartouche containing a top player's initials indicating exclusive ownership, and was earned by reaching 'London', and it meant that the other players could not step in your 'Wurlie'. Long lines of film titles and film stars' names would be chalked over swathes of the Square, and each name would be accompanied by a half finished stick man on a gibbet. Girls as well as boys would carry on these less boisterous pursuits, but there were no cross gender friendships. The girls played with each other and the boys did likewise and surprisingly little conflict would arise even when the girls were playing hopscotch and the boys were dashing around the Square in a vigorous game of 'King–he'.

The Cottage boys would also take to flicking cigarette cards against a wall in an attempt to knock down other cards leaning against it. The idea was to win cards from each other in imitation of the gambling with penny coins that some of the older boys indulged in. Gambling was illegal and adult Cottagers would sometimes break up a session, which of necessity were held in the quieter corners of the Cottages. Jimmy was never tempted to participate in 'Penny–up–the–wall' because he did not trust the older boys but he used to watch them sometimes, if they let him. From what he could gather the gamblers tossed pennies in turn towards the wall. The boy whose penny fell nearest to it would then pick up all the money, arrange the coins on the back of his hand in some ritualistic pattern for luck, and toss them in the air calling out 'heads' or 'tails'. He pocketed those pennies that landed his way up and the boy who was runner up picked up the remainder and tossed these in the air, and so on down the line. The gambler whose initial pennies had fallen furthest from the wall would be lucky to recover anything at all. Jimmy and his friends used to gamble in a not too dissimilar way with their cigarette cards, but flicking them against a wall damaged the corners and Jimmy in particular preferred to keep his best ones in good condition.

Real cigarette cards were not very common because they were no longer given away in packets of cigarettes.

Only the Turf brand still provided a card but it was of poor quality and had to be cut out. And anyway Jimmy's dad preferred to smoke Players Weights or 'Plumbers', as he liked to call them (as in 'Plumbers mates') and he could not be persuaded to change to Turf.

*

"No Jimmy, they taste like bleedin' turf as well. D'you know, I had loads of cards before the war," Jimmy's dad would reminisce, "Everybody had them. They were beautifully printed, and some of the cards were faced with silk."

Mr. Barton, being a printer's machine minder, appreciated examples of fine multi-coloured printing work.

"I had sets of film stars, sportsmen, soldiers – all sorts of animals...."

"Why did you get rid of them dad?" Jimmy asked in the hope that his father had a secret hoard of cigarette cards which he might inherit sooner rather than later.

"I didn't get rid of them Jimmy," his son's hopes were raised and then dashed, "They got lost during the war when we got bombed out of Bering Street. The whole of the back of our house was blown away. When the 'all-clear' went, your mother and me dug our way out of the Anderson shelter in the back garden – little Sally was in there with us as well. When we were allowed to go back into the house we found most of our stuff was undamaged but our suitcase had gone missing. Like the Government said we kept all our personal things and some clothes in it just in case we had to get out of the house a bit sharpish. That suitcase disappeared sharpish enough. It might have been blown away, but I reckon it was some bleedin' air raid warden who took it. There was a lot of that sort of thing going on then. Anyway my cigarette cards were in it and so were our family photographs. At least the piano was unscathed, even if it was in full view of the neighbours. We found some more rooms in Northchurch

Road and soon after that I was called up. We reported the suitcase missing but we never got it back. Bloody shame."

Jimmy comforted himself for the loss of his cigarette card inheritance with the prospect of lots of picture cards coming his way from the 'Brooke Bond' Tea Company. He had persuaded his mother to switch to 'PG Tips' tea because each quarter pound packet contained a card, and the first series of pictures were about space, that is astronomy and astrology. The Barton's tea caddy was always full because Jimmy pestered his mother to buy more and more packets of tea. He wanted to get all fifty of the Royal Astronomical Society approved cards stuck into the 'Out Into Space' album that Phillips the grocer had provided for sixpence. Jimmy would delve into his mother's shopping bag every evening looking for the oblong aromatic packets that might contain 'The Astrolabe' or the 'Eclipse of The Moon' or some other card that was missing from his album.

"Can I open these packets mum?"

"No Jimmy. Look, the caddy's full up."

"Well can I cut through the edge of the packet – I'll be able to get the card out then?"

The inner paper bag that contained the tealeaves was sealed to the lid of the outer packet. Normally this seal would only be broken when the packet was opened, but Jimmy thought that he could maintain the tea in its air tight wrapping and still get at the card situated between the inner bag and the outer wall of the packet by cutting through the latter.

"Oh do it if you must," Mrs. Barton said in exasperation.

Jimmy tried using nail scissors at first but he found one of his father's razor blades more successful. He made a neat job of the first packet of 'PG Tips' and found the card 'Orbits of The Planets'. Fortunately every packet had its card in the same position so Jimmy knew where to make the cut in the second packet. But unfortunately he not only sliced through the inner bag so that black leaves spilled on to the tablecloth, but worse than that, he also had copies of both picture cards already stuck in his album.

"Sorry mum," he said disappointedly.

"You will be Jimmy. Where am I supposed to put this tea now? You know, I let you get away with blue murder."

"I'll find you a jam jar," said Jimmy. But he could not persuade her to accept a whole row of them so that she could buy even more tea.

"We're awash with the stuff already Jimmy. You'll just have to wait for the cards like the other boys do."

But the other boys could not even get their mother's to switch to the posh 'Brooke Bond' tea, so Jimmy had no-one to swap cards with cither. Nevertheless he managed to get the full set of space cards, and the subsequent sets of British birds, animals and flowers. He used the doubles to play 'cards–up–the–wall' with Terry and Alan.

*

When it rained, which it often did in July and August, Jimmy and his friends were allowed to play in his mum's front room, even if she was out at work, and they would usually play cards. They would use Monopoly money to play Pontoon, Newmarket and Chase The Ace, and enjoy the thrill of gambling even though it was not real money. They would also play traditional games such as Snakes and Ladders, Ludo, Draughts and even Chess as well as Monopoly itself, and Jimmy even invented his own gambling game. It involved the use of a specially designed board (a piece of paper really) as well as playing cards, dice and the Monopoly money. Unfortunately the rules, long since forgotten, favoured the Banker and it was difficult for any of the other gamblers to win, and enthusiasm for Jimmy's game did not last very long, as he was usually the Banker.

The board survived for many years at the bottom of his battered Monopoly box.

In fact Jimmy produced two versions of his game. The first was called 'The Texan Gambler' which like the Monopoly board had properties marked on it. These varied from 'The Jail' valued at £150 up to the 'Lucky Oil Well' at £2100, 14 sites in all. The players placed bets on the properties and drew playing cards, and the Banker threw the dice to try to match the numbers on the cards in some convoluted way, and thereby fleece the gamblers wholesale as any self respecting Texan cowboy saloon keeper would have done. Cowboy films and comics gave the Cottage kids a broader knowledge of the geography of Texas than they had of England. Jimmy's game had references to 'The Alamo', 'Dallas', 'The Rio Grande' and 'Austin' as well as to 'The Pony Express' and 'Wells Fargo'.

The second version of his game reflected the Cottage kids growing interest in Rock and Roll music. Of course it was called 'The Rock n Roll Gambler' and it had records marked on it instead of properties. His sixteen favourite tunes at the time were written inside circles drawn around a penny coin in order of preference. He gave each tune a value ranging from £150 for 'La Dee Dah' by Jackie Dennis up to £2400 for his favourite at the time, 'Big Man' by The Four Preps, which he liked because of its clunking piano lick.

Jimmy's fascination with gambling did not go very deep. His parents did not gamble although Mrs. Barton did send the 'Vernons' football pools coupon off every week. But many other Cottagers enjoyed betting on horse and dog races. They would study form in the morning dailies and got the results from the early editions of the London evening papers, and in the meantime they would place illegal bets with the camel coated bookie who lurked in the shadows of Quinn Buildings on the opposite side of the Street. With some people gambling was an obsession. One such Cottager, a friend of Mrs. Barton, was entrusted with the Barton's thirty shillings rent money every week. She used to pay it for Mrs. Barton who was usually at work when the rent man called, but sometimes she would use it to finance a flutter. Nevertheless the rent would be paid eventually, even if it had been riding on a horse at Kempton Park first. Jimmy's mum had her suspicions about her friend but she was not bothered provided the rent was being paid, and besides, she had no letters or calls from the landlord to give her any concern. However many years later when the Cottages were compulsorily purchased for demolition under Islington Council's slum clearance programme, she was horrified at being asked by the new municipal landlords to explain her erratic record of rent payments. The new rent collectors were not as understanding as the old one had been about the Cottagers' little gaming foibles. There was to be no mucking about with the rent after this revelation and Mrs. Barton found a way to pay it in person from then on. She must have convinced the Islington housing office that the rent would never be late again because the Bartons were eventually rehoused by their new landlords in a walk–up Council flat near Canonbury Street. The shock and the shame of this episode reinforced her long held belief as a working class Tory that even if you were starving 'the rent always came first'. (See 'The End of the Cottages'.)

Jimmy's other brushes with gambling were in the seaside amusement arcades and in the fairground. He loved the glass–fronted machines in which he could flick a ball bearing around a vertical race to drop on to a series of holes paying out a premium on the gambled penny. Mostly the ball bearing bounced off the pins fixed between the holes and dropped into the losing hole at the bottom of the race. Fortunately they were usually his mother's pennies.

One August Bank Holiday Jimmy's mum and dad had taken him to the fair at Hampstead's Vale of Health. There he discovered the thrill of rolling a penny down a sloping slot on to a large board gridded with squares upon which the penny would circle until it came to a spinning rest. If the penny fell inside a square and did not touch the lines framing it, the fairground Johnny would toss some pennies, according to the number indicated in the square, in Jimmy's direction. He was elated with winning money like this and he headed straight for the roll–a–penny booths whenever he managed to get to the fair. One was held regularly at Lea Bridge Road. A few kids from Cornwall Cottages would catch a 38 bus outside Essex Road library and ride for what seemed an eternity through Dalston, Hackney Downs and Clapton to reach the fair which was set up every summer on the left bank of the River Lea. After allowing for bus fares Jimmy usually had no more than a shilling or two to gamble, but he managed to last this out for several hours by wandering around the fair in between sessions, and he had a great time. Fortunately he failed to embrace the gambling habit wholeheartedly. Unlike some he never once had to walk home penniless from the Lea. He quickly learned that the Banker always won in the end, and not only at the fair. One Saturday morning his father introduced him to the Post Office Savings Bank.

During the summer holidays the Carlton cinema held Wednesday morning picture shows as well as the regular Saturday morning ones, and Jimmy would invariably go to the show, if he got up in time. On sunny days he and his friends would also go to the local swing gardens, there were several to choose from but the one in the New River Walk behind the Carlton also had a shallow concrete boating pond. Around the pond Islington Council had used a job lot of quarry waste to create miniature stacks and cliffs where Jimmy tested his elastic–band–powered homemade stick boats among the Old Harry Rocks and The Needles.

Uniquely in summer, Jimmy and his cousin Barry would spend a day or two mooching around the City of London. They would take a picnic of boiled egg rolls and a flask of tea and catch the No.4 bus from Upper Street down to St. Paul's Cathedral. Aware of their lowly status in this world of suited gents, high heeled shoes and flunkies they felt a little intimidated and only occasionally went inside a building. Instead they wandered around Cheapside and The Bank and along the Embankment to Cleopatra's Needle, and would eat their lunch in the Embankment Gardens or on the steps of St. Paul's. They used to wander around for hours but be home before the rush hour started.

They liked to use the buses because they could look out of the windows, but on one occasion they took the underground from Bank station. The first station the train came to was London Bridge and they realised at once that they were going south rather than north. So they got off at the next stop, which was Borough. They were the only people to do so and they panicked at being south of the river on a deserted underground railway platform filled with the dirty intoxicating ozone smell of the notorious black Northern Line.

Instead of looking for the platform for the northbound trains, they dashed out of the station into Borough High Street for some fresh air. They looked at the bus numbers on the nearest bus stops but did not recognise any of them and besides they had already spent their fare money. In desperation they decided to walk home but they did not recognise any of the roads and did not even know which way was north. They were lost. In their panic they felt emboldened enough to approach a policeman for help in finding their way back to North London. He walked them along to London Bridge Station, which was nearby but well hidden, and put them on a No. 43 bus. He even gave the conductor their fares back to The Angel. And so Jimmy and Barry enjoyed their first double decker bus trip across the Thames on rush hour London Bridge, and hoped that it would not collapse under the hordes of office workers crowded on its pavements. Jimmy's mum and his Aunt Flo were worriedly waiting for the latecomers at the top of the Street. Jimmy and Barry explained what had happened and received a scolding. But after Jimmy's dad had given them a grounding in the geography of central London and in the labyrinthine nature of the London Underground system they were allowed to go on further excursions and they always kept some money in reserve.

*

Charlie Barton always took his fortnight annual holiday in August, and he would often spend the first week decorating. Cornwall Cottages were not very well maintained, and the landlords, who seemed to change annually, did not carry out any internal decorations, so when he could Mr. Barton did a little painting and wallpapering. Being a craftsman jealous of his own trade he felt a little uncomfortable about taking work away from other craftsmen. Also he did not like the idea of spending his own time and money improving someone else's property. Both of these attitudes were quite common among proletarians of his generation. However he could not afford to hire professionals, and if he did not do it himself it would never get done and Mrs. Barton would never let him forget it. The place was a 'shithole' as she put it.

On the rare occasions when Charlie Barton took up the silk purse/sow's ear challenge once again, Jimmy would volunteer his assistance, which largely involved watching and asking interminable questions.

"When your granddad moved us here from Peabody Buildings in 1913 these were the best flats around. People couldn't wait to get in them," Mr. Barton said as he smoothed out a strip of pasted wallpaper on to the bedroom wall.

He was standing on a chair and smoking a 'Weight' as he worked. Jimmy was sitting on his bed.

"There were all sorts of regulations about noise and rubbish and about using the gardens in the middle.... That's right Jimmy, all the Squares had a lovely round garden in the middle, and the Gates had real gates in them which were locked up every night to keep the riff–raff out. Now look at the place – the bleeding' riff–raff have taken over."

Jimmy listened intently as he always did when his dad talked about the old days.

"They still haven't fixed those loose slates and the wall over by the window hasn't dried out yet and here I am hanging wallpaper."

"Why don't we move dad?"

"It's not so easy Jimmy, places are hard to find and we don't want to share a house again. Me and your mother had enough of that when we got married. At least we've got two bedrooms and our own front door here. I was twelve years old when my dad died and my mum had to cope with eight of us, from baby Stanley up to Sid who was 22 and working, in a little flat just like this one – No. 57 on the first balcony it was. Your Uncle Fred left first to live with Aunt Ada and when me and your mum got married we took a spare room in the house in William Street that they shared with her father who rented it from the 'Clothworkers'. We were glad to get a room of our own but with Sally due and mum not getting on with that Ada we didn't stay long but found a couple of rooms in Bering Street. We got bombed out of there and we moved in a hurry up to Northchurch Road. I had to leave mum and Sally there when I got called up. Then they got evacuated to Yorkshire."

"Did you come back to the Cottages after that?" asked Jimmy who was carefully trimming a strip of wallpaper with Mrs. Barton's dressmaking scissors.

"We weren't sure there'd be anything left to come back to Jimmy, but we took a chance and rented this flat while we were away. They were easy to get then, and we hoped that it would still have a roof on by the time I got home and when mum felt safe enough to come back from Todmorden. Incendiary bombs set some of these top floor flats alight apparently. And all the roofs were damaged by schrapnel. No wonder they bloody leak. Jerry bombed and bloody Jerry rebuilt. Anyway mum came home and set up here, I got demobbed and got my old job back in Kentish Town and then you came along and moving never entered our heads."

"Mum says she'd like a garden," said Jimmy.

"I wouldn't fancy living on the ground Jimmy and anyway what you've never had you won't miss," said Mr. Barton, "It suits me. All my old mates are around here and people know me, and I like Islington. I was born here, in Peabody Buildings down by the 'Tib'. I'd hate it in Enfield or somewhere like that. No, this place ain't so bad."

He went into the back living room and slapped a load of paste on another strip of wallpaper which Jimmy had laid out for him on the old indispensable kitchen table.

"Of course, this roof has never been the same since Tommy climbed all over it when he was showing off to Sally. You weren't even going to school then Jimmy. He frightened the life out of your mother. He climbed all the way up the scaffolding from Pickering Street, four storeys, over the roof and down on to the balcony outside our bleedin' front door, and then he slid down all the balcony poles to the Square. He was a bit of a lad then."

Jimmy saw his sister's boyfriend Tommy Wilson in a different light after this revelation.

*

Mr. Barton did not spend all of his first week's holiday at home. He usually found time to take Jimmy out. His mum would come as well if she were not working. They sometimes went to the pictures but more usually they went sight–seeing. Jimmy's dad loved London, especially the river and its boats and the grand buildings. They would often spend an afternoon or two wandering in the British Museum, traipsing through Billingsgate, climbing the Monument, visiting the Tower of London, admiring Tower Bridge or walking along the Embankment. At other times of the year his father would take him to the Thames on the occasional Saturday morning and for a few years they went regularly to see the Lord Mayor's Show. The first time they went was when the incoming Lord Mayor was some nob in the printing industry, and Mr. Barton explained to his son what the various floats represented. But Jimmy enjoyed the horses and carriages, the military bands and the marching soldiers more than the floats.

*

For Charlie Barton's second summer holiday week the family would usually go to Ramsgate. They had tried Herne Bay, Hastings and Bognor but they found Ramsgate more to their liking. It was not as noisy and brash as Margate and Southend, and it was not suburbia–on–sea like Herne Bay and Bognor.

"During the war the American servicemen at Manston airfield were kept apart when they went on leave, the white ones couldn't go to Ramsgate and the black ones couldn't go to Margate. I know who had the best deal," said Mr. Barton as he heaved the old grey suitcase down the stairs of Cornwall Cottages.

The case contained all that was necessary for a week at the seaside for the three of them, Sally had stopped going on family holidays some years before, and it was bulging against its fully extended expanding straps. Jimmy looked at his father's familiar forearm straining against the weight of the case and at his thick wrist and at the ganglion of veins on the back of his hand. Although he was a craftsman printer Mr. Barton had to do a fair amount of physical work, handling reams of paper and maintaining and operating his three colour lithographic printing machine whose rollers needed dismantling and washing down after each run. Jimmy wondered if he would ever have arms like his dad, and he especially admired the four bluish tattoos on his forearms.

"I had these done down The Gut in Valletta when things were a bit quieter after the Blitz. The old King had just given the George Cross to the people of Malta and I had a George Cross put on this arm and a Maltese Cross put on the other. And this one is the badge of the Royal Artillery, 'Ubique' means 'everywhere' Jimmy, and this heart has your mum's name through it, see?"

Charlie Barton wet his fingers and rubbed the tattoos so that the fading colours stood out better. Jimmy thought that he would like a tattoo one–day but it would have to mean something, like his dad's did.

They turned out of the Gate and made their way down the Street, round the 'Bottom', past Charlie Mutton school and so to Shepperton Walk and the George IV pub where the 'Grey Green' and 'Orange' coaches made their Saturday morning Islington pick ups. Several coaches were already there but not the one for Ramsgate. It was a little late and when it turned the corner out of Popham Road a cheer went up. The coach was already half full with holidaymakers from Edmonton and Holloway. It had got held up in traffic at Nag's Head. The Bartons found their seats and Jimmy sat by the window next to his mum. The driver said he had to make one more stop at New Cross on the Old Kent Road.

The ride through London was one of the favourite parts of Jimmy's long anticipated holiday at the seaside, and he squashed his face against the window as the coach sped down New North Road and over the canal bridge.

"There's Bering Street where we used to live until we got bombed out – and over there, behind those houses, is Bridport Place where I grew up, it's all gone now. None of the family live in Hoxton anymore. They've all moved miles away except for little Auntie Alice and Uncle Bert, and your Auntie Violet's family."

Martha Barton had five married sisters and an older, bachelor brother who had died a few years before at the age of 49, largely it was said because he was left lying on a coster's barrow overnight down the side of the Bacchus pub, the worse for drink, and he caught pneumonia.

"You know Jimmy, your Uncle Jim never forgave me for having the dog put down. I suppose Rex was his dog really – he doted on it. It was during that bloody war. He was in the army in the Middle East. Your grandmother had died years before this, God rest her. Betty, May and me were all married and so that left Violet keeping house in Bridport Place for your granddad and your Aunt Eileen and Aunt Addy who were both schoolgirls then. Violet came round to me in Bering Street and told me that she couldn't cope any longer with the girls because they kept running out after the dog whenever the air raid sirens went off and the planes came over. He would bark and carry on and they couldn't control him. Your granddad wouldn't do anything. He was a sullen old bugger. I was really worried about Eileen and Addy getting hit by schrapnel or worse and so I took the dog to the PDSA and told them about the problem and they reluctantly agreed to put him down. It broke my heart. My brother never forgave me. I was the only one he didn't have a present for from Palestine. He never had a friendly word for me afterwards. I could cope with that alright, but what upset me was he never had any time for Sally or for you come to that."

Jimmy's mum had an intense sense of duty and she never flinched from doing what she thought was necessary. It was this sense of duty and her unshakeable honesty that was a constant source of exasperation for her husband but it was on this rock that the happiness of the Barton family was founded.

The coach passed Dawsons and carried on to Moorgate and the Bank, through territory that Jimmy knew quite well from his many excursions to the City with his cousin and his dad. The holiday truly began when they eventually crossed the Thames into the terra incognita of South London. As the coach rolled across London Bridge Jimmy stood on his seat to get a better view of the Tower of London and Tower Bridge and of the cranes of St. Catherine's and Irongate Wharf beyond. He jumped when he realised that they were cruising down Borough High Street where he and Barry had got lost earlier in the month. The Ramsgate coach must have passed this way on previous holidays, but when he and Barry had emerged in a panic from the bowels of the Northern Line Jimmy had not recognised it.

The trip through the south–east London suburbs was slow and boring but once they had passed Bexley on the A2 Jimmy relaxed and let the hedges, fields and orchards and the Kentish ribbon development flash by. The holidaymakers unceasingly consumed sweets and fruit and the coach was permeated with the nauseating smell of hard–boiled eggs and sardines. At least one kid would be sick on these trips, but Jimmy never succumbed, to the relief of his parents.

The journey took about four hours, but it always seemed longer than that. They stopped at a 'Half Way House', usually a big road–side pub full of coach parties where the queues for the 'Ladies' were long enough to allow the men to get a few drinks in. Jimmy's dad knew all about 'half way houses' because he had played the piano in many of them on summer pub excursions from the Packington Arms.

"They would've had me playing on the coach as well if they could've got the piano on board," he said as he handed Jimmy a bottle of cherryade and a straw.

The 'Half Way House' to Ramsgate could be on either side of the bottleneck of Rochester Bridge depending on where the coach driver got the best backhander. Rochester, with the other Medway towns, formed the biggest urban area on the A2 outside of London and it took some getting through. Then came Sittingbourne and Faversham and eventually the coach was speeding through the Isle of Thanet cabbage fields.

From the treeless elevated Thanet plateau they had their first sweeping view of the sea running southwards from Pegwell Bay towards Sandwich. Jimmy's excitement mounted when he glanced down a steep Ramsgate street and saw the sea at the bottom seeming to reach up to the rooftops. The coach turned into a large dusty parking lot behind the High Street and the Barton family joined the melee of slightly anxious passengers waiting for the driver to unload their cases from the back. Mr. Barton gave him a silver coin as he grabbed the suitcase and led the way between the rows of hot coaches to the pavement that was crowded with Londoners and their impedimenta waiting for buses and taxis. The Barton's boarding house was within walking distance and they followed the directions sent to them by the landlady whose address Mr. Barton had found in the 'Dalton's Weekly' many months before.

Jimmy and his mum and dad always shared a room when on holiday, just as they did in Cornwall Cottages. Every morning the landlady would knock on their door and leave a jug of hot water outside for them to wash with. There was a big ceramic bowl on a marble–topped washstand in a corner of their room for the purpose. Each day after breakfast they would go out and not return until bedtime. If it was not wet or too cold they would spend much of the day on Ramsgate's wide sandy beach on the east side of the harbour wall, where Jimmy would dig in the sand all day. Mr. and Mrs. Barton would hire deck chairs and doze and read the 'Daily Express', and Mrs. Barton would knit. She would cover herself up and wear a hat but Mr. Barton liked to sun bathe in his vest and trousers. He loved to soak up the heat whenever he could.

"I'll get some tea Martha – you coming Jimmy?"

They would bring back a tray of tea things from a beach cafe and some ice creams, as Mrs. Barton was inordinately fond of ice cream.

Jimmy could not swim and was uncomfortably shy about exposing his body on the beach. Martha Barton could not swim either and had no desire to learn but Mr. Barton had been a good swimmer as a young man. However, the cold North Sea held little attraction for him as he had spent two years swimming in the balmy grottoes of Malta, courtesy of the War Department. He had taken Jimmy a couple of times to the 'Tib', but Jimmy did not enjoy it. He was not athletic, and since moving to Charlie Mutton Juniors he had grown a little plumper every year. His mum and dad thought that he would grow out of this shy puppy fat stage and would learn to swim when the time was right.

"You should get in the water with the other kids, you'd love it," said Mr. Barton as he and Jimmy paddled in the wash of the Ramsgate waves.

"It's perishing dad, I'd sooner play on the beach."

Mr. Barton had rolled up his trousers to his knees and his ivory white feet looked painfully cold in the spume.

"It makes your toes turn up alright," said Mr. Barton, "It's nothing like the Med. I used to swim for hours in the sea when I was in Malta. It was really warm. Before the Blitz started our sergeant used to take us down to the rocks – we never saw a beach – for PT and swimming. The first time we went he asked our platoon if anyone could swim, and me and this Scots bloke put our hands up. I was quite proud of my swimming – I'd spent years round the 'Tib' as a kid, and I'd got medals from school. I used to have eyes like an albino and skin like a prune. 'Right', says the sergeant, 'I want you two to teach the rest how to swim and I don't want anyone drowned either.' So I spent all those PT sessions and a lot of my spare time swimming in the Med. I tell you it's got to be a proper heatwave before you'll get me in the bleedin' North Sea."

Mr. and Mrs. Barton had to entice Jimmy away from the sands with the promise of rides in the amusement ground called 'Merrie England' that sheltered below Ramsgate's east cliff. His favourite rides were the 'Dodgems' and the 'Ghost Train'. Once on his return from holiday he had attempted to make his own ghost tunnel in the front room using all the furniture and the bed sheets, some torches and a few Guy Fawkes masks. Mrs. Barton was not too pleased when she came home from work to find her parlour turned into an assault course for Jimmy and an assortment of ghoulish friends.

He also enjoyed the arcades where he liked to watch the moving tableaux of the penny automatons. He was transfixed by the ghosts and devils that popped out of the graves of the 'Haunted Churchyard', and by the mummies that crept up on a topee'd Howard Carter figure in the 'Curse of The Pharaohs'. After one of these brushes with the world of automation he came home with the intention of building his own machines, but he only got as far as making one out of a shoe box, some cardboard and a cotton reel. It dispensed cigarettes to his father who had to put a penny in a slot to catapult out one of his own cigarettes. The machine proved to be very temperamental and this did nothing to relieve Mr. Barton's need for nicotine and he soon refused to co–

operate with it, and he kept his cigarettes to himself, and his pennies.

They would often have lunch in the fish and chip restaurant at the end of the eastern arm of Ramsgate's outer harbour. On the way they would study the anglers' catches and look into the holds of the rusty fishing boats moored below the quay and step around the nets lying out to dry on the quayside. The restaurant was built on concrete stilts above the widened end of the harbour breakwater. From the restaurant they could watch the boats bounce in and out of the choppy harbour entrance below the windows. The town looked lovely across the water. It came down from the terracotta and chalk cliffs as if it were about to tumble into the inner harbour.

Another of their favourite haunts in Ramsgate was Pelosi's ice cream parlour on the harbour front where they would eat 'celebrated' ice cream, validated by the many certificates for 'ice cream excellence' that lined the wall behind the counter. The ice cream parlour was decorated in panels of pastel pink and green enamel, with lots of mirrors trimmed with gold and silver, and glass shelves supporting pyramids of silver dishes and lines of glass gondolas used for ice cream concoctions. Eating ice cream to the accompaniment of the hiss and rumble of the espresso coffee machine was one of the gastronomic highlights of Jimmy Barton's holiday, another was the hot dog he would have on the way back to the digs when the day was over.

During their week at Ramsgate Mr. and Mrs. Barton would get relief from the beach by dragging Jimmy off on excursions. Sometimes they would take a bus trip to Margate but mostly they would walk across the tamed cliff tops that ran east and west from the harbour. The walk along the east cliff led past Dumpton Park and on to Broadstairs, which had a lovely beach but little else to attract the Bartons. It was a bit too precious for them. On the way back they would stop in King George VI Park to relax and to let Jimmy have a kick around.

The cliff top walk westwards from Ramsgate began with a climb up the road that crossed the reinforced cliff face rising from the back of the inner harbour. Bulbous terracotta balusters topped with a wide cream coloured parapet protected the edge of the road. The lampposts along the balustrade were strung with coloured lights. Jimmy liked these old chalk and terracotta cliffs, especially at night when the lights came on to join hundreds of others lining the quays of the inner harbour. The road turned inland at the top where the wide tarmac promenade and grassy tops of West Cliff began. Below lay the wide expanse of rocks and pools where Jimmy would often spend hours catching shrimps and crabs or a starfish or two. Underneath the promenade was a theatre, built into a cleft in the cliffs, where they could get tickets for a performance of 'Old Time Music Hall'.

The West Cliff walk led eventually to Pegwell Bay, two miles from Ramsgate. On the way Jimmy would run off to the railings to look down on the rocks and sand, and then back to the grassy mounds near the bowling green to roll over and over, and then up ahead to wait by an ice cream kiosk – just like a happy dog. They would usually stop for a cup of tea by the boating pond on West Cliff and sometimes for a drink in Pegwell in the pub garden, which was precariously perched on the cliff top overlooking the bay.

Pegwell Bay was flat and expansive and so shallow that the receding tide exposed a mile of muddy sand dotted with cocklers and bait diggers. The low cliff tops that ran from the village along the eastern end of the bay were of clay rather than chalk. Jimmy's mother would not let him clamber up and down the many gullies worn in the cliff faces by kids and the weather. However he would be content to pick some early blackberries or to run ahead to where the cliff top path came down to the head of the bay. Here they would spend an hour or two on the beach below the sea wall at the back of the big cafe, which was the only amenity at Pegwell Bay. The beach was white with crushed cockleshells, and when he was not paddling Jimmy would make patterns out of the shells and collect specimens in his bucket to take home as a reminder of the holidays. Before walking back to Ramsgate they would always make a pilgrimage to see the Viking longboat, aground on concrete trestles set in the grass beside the bay. It was a scaled down replica that a crew of young Danes had sailed over from Denmark in 1949 to celebrate the ancient invasions of this shore by some of our more warlike ancestors.

The Barton's last evening in Ramsgate usually coincided with the open air concert and firework display at Ellington Park and they would go back to the boarding house earlier than usual to get brushed up for the show and to get packed. Jimmy would moan and dawdle on the way up from the beach. While there was still some sunlight left he wanted to carry on digging in the sand or at least spend some pennies in the arcade.

"Come on Jimmy, we've got a lot to do if you want to see the fireworks tonight."

"Can't we go in the amusements for a bit?"

"No, come on."

He ran his spade along the railings and over the flint and pebbledash garden walls of the houses on the way.

"Stop doing that Jimmy. You're giving me a headache."

Jimmy's spade had knocked a few shells off the garden walls and he stopped to pick them up. He had not seen shells like these before on the beach and he popped them into his bucket to join a few cockle and whelk shells he had collected earlier. As he walked he looked out for more shells and knocked them off the walls with deft swipes of his spade.

"Now what are you doing?"

"I'm collecting shells mum."

"Haven't you got enough already Jimmy?" There's a bleedin' bag full back at Mrs. T's," said Mr. Barton.

Jimmy ran on ahead so that he could collect shells in peace, and by the time his mum and dad reached him outside the digs his bucket was full. Once inside their room Mrs. Barton organised water for washing and began the packing.

"You'll have to put all your shells together in your bag and carry them home yourself, there's no room in the suitcase."

He put his bucket on the floor next to his bed beside his school duffle bag, which was already a quarter full of sand, shells and pebbles.

Later that evening the Bartons joined the crowd of people streaming into Ellington Park and sat on the grass to listen to the brass band that struck up as dusk began to settle. At the end of the field was a fenced off section containing mysterious wooden structures with groups of men standing furtively by. Jimmy thought that fireworks were the most glamorous and exciting things ever invented and he was impatient for the music to end and for the display to begin. Eventually the music ended with two jingoistic tunes, 'Land of Hope and Glory' and 'Rule Britannia', and then the fireworks began.

The people in the crowd jostled for position in the dark to watch the display. Mr. Barton lifted Jimmy on to his shoulders. All the dads in the crowd had similar additions to their upper torsos. Jimmy was mesmerised by the colours and patterns, the noise and the smoke. The Guy Fawkes Night fireworks down the Street were not a patch on these. Jimmy wanted the fireworks to go on all night but he knew the end had come when, out of the gloom, the fireworks on the wooden gantry came into glaring crackling life to reveal a glorious pyrotechnic Union Jack and the dazzling white injunction 'God Save The Queen'. The applause, the flag and the words died away bit by bit to leave a pall of smoke wafting around the field. With glare blinded eyes the Bartons shuffled along with the crowd and out of the park gates. Jimmy felt a little sad now that the fireworks and the holiday were over and he traipsed solemnly back to the digs. Even a final hot–dog failed to dispel his gloom completely.

"Jimmy, wake up dear, we're going home this morning – lots to do," his mother said as she touched his shoulder. It was then that she saw the shells on the headboard of his bed.

"Have you been playing with those shells in here, you'll get sand everywhere?"

"No mum."

"Ooer, it's moving. Look!"

She clapped her hand to her mouth when she saw two tiny eyestalks and a snail's head twitch into view from under one of the shells. Jimmy turned around and saw that his headboard had five or six shells stuck to it and some of them were moving. He got out of bed and carefully put his feet on to the floor so as not to step on the dozen or so snails that were nonchalantly wandering across the lino.

"It's alright mum. I think they're all over this side of the room."

"What do you mean, it's alright? How many are there?"

"Well the bucket was full yesterday," he picked it up, "It's not now. They must have climbed out in the night mum."

"What.... Where are they?"

"Your mother will have a fit with her leg up, Jimmy, she can't abide snails," laughed Mr. Barton.

"That's spiders, and it's not funny Charlie, we've got to find them."

When you are not looking for things they can pass unnoticed, but when the Bartons set their eyes to snail seeking mode they could see them everywhere. Well not quite everywhere, they were at least concentrated on Jimmy's side of the room.

"I could have trod on one," shivered Mrs. Barton.

"Didn't you notice the things were snails Jimmy? You are a silly little sod," said Mr. Barton.

"No, sorry dad. They weren't moving at all yesterday. The shells looked empty, or at least they weren't full up to the top. I thought they only had sand and dirt in them."

There was a knock on the door.

"It's Mrs. T with the jug of hot water," whispered Mrs. Barton, "Don't let her in now Charlie, she'll have apoplexy if she sees these snails."

Mr. Barton opened the door.

"Thanks Mrs. T. Yes that's right, the coach leaves at ten so we'll be off in an hour or so."

He resisted the temptation to do a little flirting.

"She's not such a bad old stick for a landlady," he said as he carried the jug to the washstand, "Look at this, one of the cheeky little sods is staring up at me out of the bleedin' basin."

Mrs. Barton could not stifle a smile.

"You Jimmy, I'm putting you in charge of these things and I want them all back in that bucket in double quick time, d'you hear?"

Jimmy pulled out his bed and the chest of drawers to hunt down the fugitive molluscs. They had spread out in centrifugal waves from where the bucket had sat between Jimmy's bed and the wall, as if they could not stand anymore to be cooped up together like that. Jimmy picked them off the floor, the walls, the backs, fronts and sides of the furniture, and off the underside of chairs, and one or two he had to knock off the ceiling with his fishing net.

"I'd better not find one of those in my shoes," said Mr. Barton as he shaved at the washstand with one eye looking out for peripatetic snails.

Jimmy looked inside his dad's brown brogues, "All clear dad."

When they were all washed and ready to go they made a final search for the sneakiest snails. The ones that had been recaptured were continually trying to escape from the bucket again but Jimmy had their escape routes covered.

"How're we doing?" asked Mr. Barton.

"The bucket's not full yet dad. They won't keep still."

"Poor little blighters, they must be hungry," said Mrs. Barton, "there's nothing for them to eat in here."

"Nothing 'cept us," winked Mr. Barton, "They might've crept up on us in the night and done us in if we hadn't woke up in time."

"Horrible," said Mrs. Barton.

"I don't think they eat meat dad," Jimmy paused, "They don't, do they?"

"We'd have been done for if they did."

"Well I can't find anymore," said Mrs. Barton.

"We'd better get a move on then," said Mr. Barton. He paused, "Mrs. T might get a few shocks when she sweeps in here next time. I hope she don't do it in her stockinged feet."

Mr. and Mrs. Barton guffawed at the thought of Mrs. T dressed in her stockings and not much else and standing on a chair besieged by snails. Jimmy's mum wiped up a few slimy tell tale trails with the face flannel, dropped a last desperado into the heaving bucket and gathered up the coats and bags. Mr. Barton took up the suitcase, and Jimmy swung his duffle bag on to his shoulder and picked up the bucket.

"Don't you dare trip up with those things."

They went out into the hall and Mr. Barton knocked on Mrs. T's kitchen door.

Mrs. Barton whispered, "Jimmy you go outside now and wait for us on the pavement."

"But mum."

"Now! Jimmy."

He went, but not before pointing to the snail that had appeared from under the door of their room.

"We'll be off now Mrs. T," said Mr. Barton.

"We had a lovely time," said Mrs. Barton and she rushed her husband into the street, "Mustn't miss that coach."

They walked sharply away, snails leaping out of the bucket like lemmings. However most of them set up a new colony on the scrubby wasteland beside the coach park where Jimmy had finally dumped them.

"How embarrassing," said Mrs. Barton as she found her seat in the coach, "We can't go back there again. What will that poor lady think of us?"

"No harm done Martha," said Mr. Barton as he sat down next to her, "Hold on. I think I can see one on the back of your neck."

Martha Barton shrieked. The other passengers on the coach looked around at her.

"It's all right," she called out, "The old man's only tickling me."

On the journey home Mr. Barton set up lots of different scenarios involving snails and Mrs. T, most of which were rude, and the pair of them were still laughing when they got off the coach at Shepperton Road.

GUY FAWKES

Jimmy and Terry were sitting on the bottom step of the new brick built dustbin enclosure, which had been put up in the middle of the Square as a new eyesore. They were tired of running up and down the steps, and of climbing on to the concrete roof slab, and they were now contemplating what to do next.

They were not obstructing any Cottagers from getting to the refuse chute door at the top of the steps, because the ground floor tenants usually used the big bin–store door instead. The padlock was missing, and they tipped their rubbish, or most of it, over the edge of the tall steel container which festered inside. Once a week the Islington bin men wheeled out the containers from all the four new bin enclosures built in and around the Square, and noisily rolled them through the Gate to their waiting refuse vehicle. Jimmy and Terry had looked on in disbelief when they first saw one of these containers being hoisted 20 feet into the air by this remarkable machine. Its complete rear section along with the container, gripped in seemingly robotic arms, was pushed up on shiny steel hydraulic rams. The rubbish was tipped out of the container and into the bowels of the cart. The driver jiggled the controls, and the rams shook the container as if it weighed nothing, to make sure that it was empty.

Terry and Jimmy appreciated these extraordinarily noisy technological improvements to the Cottagers' refuse collection service. It was far more exciting to watch this than to watch the bin men in earlier days. They just used to shovel the rubbish from the old half–height brick boxes at the bottom of the chutes into small galvanised bins, which they lifted on to their leather–clad backs and carried out to the Street. There the rubbish was tipped into the side of a far less technologically fascinating, but infinitely more attractive refuse vehicle that had curved sliding doors like a huge bread bin. Occasionally the bin men found a rat and chased it across the Square in the hope of crowning it with a shovel.

On this particular overcast morning there was no refuse collection due, and Terry and Jimmy just sat on the cold bottom step of the bin enclosure wandering what to do with themselves. It was the first day of the autumn half term holiday, which meant that they were burning up with firework fever. All their available cash had already been spent on fireworks, and now they sat penniless in the middle of the Cornwall Square. Jimmy heard his name being called and looked up to the top balcony where old Mrs. Smith, who lived alone in the flat two doors along from him, was gesticulating across the washing lines. He got up and ran over to the corner of the Square.

"Yes Mrs. Smith?" he called.

"Jimmy, be a dear and get me a few errands would you?" asked Mrs. Smith, "I've got to wait in for the gas man."

"Sure," he shouted, "What d'ya want?"

Down came some coins wrapped in a shopping list, followed by a battered shopping bag. He picked them up, waved to Mrs. Smith, and walked over to Terry.

"Fancy coming up Essex Road with me?" he asked.

"Got nuffin' better to do," said Terry, and they walked out of the Gate knowing that the going rate for getting errands for neighbours was about sixpence, and that they would soon be solvent again.

They walked past Edinburgh Cottages, and round the short curve of Elder Walk where Morris's assistant was sharpening knives on the sandstone doorstep of a house long since bombed to oblivion. The fishmonger's knives were gradually completing Goering's unfinished business, because the doorstep was wearing very thin. Morris's was the first shop on the near side of Essex Road and stood next to the Half Moon at the very top of the Street. Beyond the fishmonger's past Elder Walk came Fred Holloway's fruit stall by the bomb ruins, and this was followed by Boundy the butcher's, Phillips the grocer's, the Home and Colonial store, Geoffrey Martin's haberdashery shop and Jimmy's first call, Vinns the baker's. He joined the queue inside the baker's shop waiting for a fresh batch of loaves to be brought in from the back. The smell of bread in the shop was intoxicating. The trays of loaves arrived and were slid into the steel racking behind the twin counters. The queue soon dispersed carrying off half of the late morning's bake. Jimmy tucked the large crusty twist, in its sheets of tissue paper, under his arm but it was too hot and he popped it into the shopping bag.

Because Jimmy's mother worked, she only managed to get hot bread on Saturday morning, and only if her factory was not on overtime. On those Saturdays, Jimmy always had the topper from the loaf with a wedge of butter rapidly melting through it. There was no taste to match it. However, The temptation to rip open Mrs. Smith's loaf and eat some of the soft steamy and yeasty interior was successfully resisted, and Jimmy and Terry moved on to Day's the greengrocer's. Day's corner shop was open to the street on two sides and was floored with bare boards. Fruit and salad stuff was laid out on the sloping tops of the brightly painted wooden counters under which were kept piles of potatoes, onions and turnips. When Jimmy was little his mum would have to oik him out of the potatoes whenever her attention was elsewhere. But this time Jimmy had legitimate business in the shop and posed no danger to Day's potatoes. Soon Mrs. Smith's bag was half full of King Edwards, a few onions and two huge Bramley apples, with the bread on the top of course.

"This bleedin' bag's heavy," said Jimmy as they walked back to Phillips the grocer's, "Can't you carry it for a bit?"

"They're your bloody errands," said Terry.

"Tell yer what," said Jimmy as they reached Phillips, "You carry it as far as the Gate and you can have half of whatever she gives me. Fair enough?"

"She might not give you anything."

"Yes she will."

"Alright. But she better 'ad."

So Jimmy bought Mrs. Smith's groceries in Phillips, and Terry carried the bag as far as the Gate where Jimmy took over and carried it up the three flights of stairs to the top balcony.

"Oh thank you Jimmy, you are a love," said Mrs. Smith when Jimmy handed over the heavy bag and the change, "Those stairs just about crease me."

Jimmy thought, "Yeah, me and all," as he pocketed sixpence for his pains.

"I 'spect you're looking forward to Firework Night," she said.

"Best night of the year Mrs. Smith," Jimmy grinned.

"My grandchildren are getting excited as well, they're coming over to see the bonfires this year."

Jimmy ran down the stairs to Terry who was waiting in the Gate.

"What she give you?"

"A tanner."

"Great!"

"Let's get some bangers."

They went down the 'Bottom' to Buddings the newsagent's who had been selling Benwell fireworks since the end of September. They were displayed in glass cases on the shop counter, brought out once a year especially for the purpose. The high shelves at the back of the shop were lined with mysterious boxes of fireworks, but the display cases at the front were full of the wonderful objects themselves. They were laid out in neat colourful rows, Roman candles, volcanoes, snow storms, rockets, aeroplanes, squibs, fountains, traffic lights, Catherine wheels, jumping Jacks and bangers of course. The bangers were in boxes according to price, a penny, penny ha'penny, tuppence, and thrupence, the higher the price the thicker was the cardboard tube containing the gunpowder and the louder the bang. Terry and Jimmy looked longingly at the fireworks but eventually bought six penny bangers.

Jimmy put his bangers in the top pocket of his jacket where they were less likely to get damaged. The telltale blue paper twists of the fuses stood out like a row of medal ribbons. Terry walked ahead to the bottom of the Street, at the corner of Albany Cottages. Jimmy was ten yards behind Terry and as he turned the corner he saw a banger sparking away on the pavement. He stepped back smartly as the thing exploded with a satisfying crack. He took out his matches, which every kid carried at this time of year, lit one of his bangers and charged round the corner once more holding the fizzing firework at arms length behind him. Terry was still laughing a few yards up the Street, and he dashed off when he saw Jimmy coming. Jimmy threw the banger at the fleeing Terry and it rolled in the gutter and exploded.

"That's two good ones," said Terry, "These bangers ain't bad at all. Look at that, it's split wide open."

Terry picked up the dead firework, blackened and warm and smelling of sulphurous promise. The loudest bangers exploded in this way, the least satisfying ones just blew the plug or the fuse casing out of the ends with a loud 'phut'. A sash went up and an Albany woman stuck her head out of her ground floor bedroom window. Jimmy and Terry, being Cornwall kids were not familiar with the temperament of Albany Cottagers, and so they ran off up the Street followed by some advice about what they could do with bloody Guy Fawkes. They turned sharply into the Queens Gate and looked back down the street. All clear.

They got their money's worth out of the remaining bangers, which kept them occupied for the rest of the day. They dropped one down a drain hole to achieve a less than satisfying deep 'wumph' sound. They set off another banger in a crack in the mortar of the staircase wall in the Queens' gate, hoping unsuccessfully to make a bigger hole. They launched their fifth banger into the big puddle in the dank Airey between Cornwall and Queens Cottages. It fizzed along like a slow torpedo, sparks bubbling through the water, and the explosion caused a minor waterspout and an echo bouncing between the parallel blocks of flats. Jimmy and Terry got out of the Airey in a hurry and took their last banger over the bomb ruins on the other side of the Street.

A bonfire was being built on the widest part of the ruins between the Street and Britannia Row, which ran parallel to it. A group of older children were piling up planks, old furniture, chestnut palings and all kinds of boxes under the supervision of Raymond Bishop. Peter Sullivan, the young hard case from Quinn Buildings was organising the bomb site bonfire, but while he was at work Raymond was standing in. Jimmy and Terry knew that they would not be forced to help with building the bonfire, as this was a privilege reserved for Peter Sullivan's gang and hangers–on.

"Piss off you two," said Raymond as they came up to the mountain of combustibles.

"We're just looking," said Terry.

"Well don't," said Raymond, and he shoved Terry in the chest.

So they sloped off to the bottom of the ruins by the side wall of Albert's sweet shop. The shop was a converted terraced house whose neighbours on both sides had been flattened by the Luftwaffe. Why Albert's was spared the Cottagers could not imagine, as he was a miserable bugger who diddled the kids if he could. When he died his wife carried on diddling and the shop became known as Peggy's. The ruins next to Albert's back yard were in the shadow of the high back wall of the hall belonging to St. James' Church, and there were still puddles of rainwater lying around, not yet evaporated. Terry and Jimmy got down on their hands and knees and chose a likely puddle for enlarging. Firstly they piled up dirt and stones into a line along one edge of the puddle, and then they dug a shallow channel from a slightly higher puddle which then drained into the first making it twice as deep. After half an hour of exercising admirable civil engineering skills they were ready to breach the dammed puddle. Jimmy gently pushed his last banger low down into the dry side of the dirt dam and Terry began to whistle the 'Dam Busters' March'. He lit the fuse and Jimmy spread his arms and made growling noises like a squadron of Lancaster bombers.

It was a perfect hit. The banger had been set at the right depth. The three inches of dirt and mud above it were blasted away, mostly into the faces of the intrepid Lancaster pilots, and the water began to flow through the breach dragging more of the dam with it. The trickle became a torrent which flooded the Rhur Valley next to Albert's wall. Barnes Wallis would have been proud.

"Hey, they've got bangers," Raymond yelled as he and his bonfire builders came running across the ruins.

"It was our last one Ray, honest," squawked Jimmy as he and Terry dashed over the Street and into the Queens' Gate. Raymond's squadron completed what the Lancasters had begun. Using broken bricks and handfuls of stones they finished off the dam on the Rhur. High on destruction and with mud spattered legs they went back to the task of building the biggest bonfire the Street had ever seen.

After the bombing raid Terry and Jimmy went home to their respective flats in Cornwall Cottages. They were cold and filthy but pleased with the first day of Guy Fawkes week. Jimmy's mother had just got home from work and she sat him down in front of the fire in the front room and attacked him with a wet flannel.

"You've been over those bloody bomb ruins again, and look at those shoes. What am I going to do with you?"

"Do you want any errands doing mum?" Jimmy smiled.

After tea Jimmy pulled out the biscuit tin from under his bed where he kept his collection of fireworks. He had been buying them in ones and twos on his way home from school for several weeks past and every day he gloated over them as if they were pirates' treasure. He was overcome by the smell of them, by the graphite–like dusty feel of them, by their firm rounded shapes, by their names and colours and by their promise of unknown fiery wonders. He arranged them on the floor in height order, and then in the order in which he intended to let them off on Firework Night, leaving his favourites until last, and then in price order. Finally he put them away safely under his bed once more. Jimmy was obsessed.

For several days Raymond and his wood scavengers had been scouring the neighbourhood for anything that would burn. Much of the bonfire that had already been built on the

161

bomb ruins consisted of furniture donated by a few Cottagers who had taken the opportunity of the bonfire season to replace worn out sofas and chairs. But such donations were never enough, and searching parties were sent out every day with instructions to bring back more and more, even if this meant raiding other bonfires in neighbouring streets and fighting off rivals.

As the bonfire grew Raymond became more agitated. He took his responsibilities seriously. The bonfire would be the centrepiece of the great pagan outpouring of Guy Fawkes' Night. He had to post more guards around the rising tide of wood to fend off outside raiding parties, and he was relieved when Peter Sullivan's gang took over guard duties during the hours of darkness.

Two days after Jimmy and Terry had re–enacted the exploits of Guy Gibson's squadron, and two days before Guy Fawkes Night itself, the great bonfire had overtaken the Street record of 15 feet in height and it was still growing. The kids down the Street were proud of the mountain erupting 50 yards away from the Queens' Gate. Even those kids, who were too young or too far down the pecking order to be actually involved in the orogenic activities, were proud. Jimmy and his friends were also proud members of the great excluded, but they were not bothered, as they did not fancy a daily dose of aggravation from Raymond.

On this momentous day Jimmy, Terry and Alan were playing Monopoly on the floor of Jimmy's front room when they heard the bells of a fire engine. Although not a rare sound, as some Cottagers tended to neglect getting their chimneys swept and were always setting them alight, fire engine bells would immediately attract the attention of any child within ear shot. The three boys grabbed their coats and ran around the top balcony of Cornwall Cottages.

"You don't reckon someone's set the bonfire alight, do you?" said Jimmy with a mixture of unease and excitement.

They rushed down the three flights of stairs that led to the Gate, two at a time, except for Jimmy who could not force himself to do this since he had badly twisted his ankle going down two at a time a few years before. He was the last to dash into the Street.

"It's a fire engine alright," Terry said to Jimmy as he caught up, "It's parked by the bomb ruins, but I don't think the bonfire is burning. See?"

Adults as well as kids were gathering around the engine, which was also accompanied by an open backed lorry. Several blue clad, booted and helmeted firemen were in deep discussion with a small group of Cottagers, or 'know–it–alls' as Jimmy's dad would have called them.

"We've got our orders. It's a fire risk," the fire chief was saying.

Of course it is," said one 'know–it–all', "We're gonna set it alight in two days time."

"No you ain't! We are!" yelled Raymond from the direction of the bonfire where his band of wood marauders stood guard, "We built it and we're gonna burn it."

"We'll see about that," threatened the fire chief as he ordered his reluctant men to approach the bonfire. Another indignant 'know–it–all' approached the chief.

"Come on mate, these kids 'ave bin 'ard at it all week. You can't tell me you never 'ad a bonfire when you was their age."

"You tell 'im 'arry," urged a female onlooker.

"Just 'cos your wearing bloody Wellingtons and a bleedin' great 'at, you reckon you can come down 'ere and boss us all about."

"You tell 'im 'arry."

"And where was you when Jerry was trying to set the whole place on fire? Stopping kids from lighting matches, were you?"

"You tell 'im 'arry," said Jimmy mischievously.

163

As much as Jimmy, Terry and Alan found this adult set–to quite absorbing but as unfathomable as most of the rows down the Street, their attention was suddenly gained by Raymond and his gang. They had taken up stones from the ruins and were throwing them at the firemen who had begun to dismantle the great pyre. The young Davids were being egged on by the onlookers lining the pavement, and soon the firemen were forced to retreat to their engine for protection from the onslaught. The chief said he would be back and ordered his vehicles to move off, to the cheers and laughter of his tormentors.

"That was pretty good," said Terry as he led the way back through the Cornwall Square and up to Jimmy's flat, to resume their marathon Monopoly tournament.

"That Raymond was taking a bit of a chance," said Alan

"At least he saved the bonfire," said Jimmy.

But later that day the firemen returned with a posse of police who chased away Raymond's Promethean Guards into their secret Cottage hideaways. The bonfire was dismantled and removed from the ruins.

Jimmy and Terry had a good pitch next to the chip shop, just around the top of the Street in Essex Road by the bus stop. Earlier in the week they had invested in a papier–mâché mask from Buddings and had stuck it to a paper–stuffed stocking that had last seen service on Mrs. Barton's left leg. And with the help of other discarded remnants, otherwise destined for the rag and bone man over the road, they had fabricated a passable Guy. Unfortunately they had no pram or cart to wheel the Guy around in. Jimmy had carried it up the Street every evening since they had made it, and suffered interminable comments about his poor little brother who looked as if he were at death's door. They were feeling a bit down as they sat the Guy up against the pillar–box, opposite the bus stop.

"You can't have Bonfire Night without a bonfire," reasoned Terry.

"You'd think those firemen would enjoy putting out bonfires, wouldn't you? There's not much point being a fireman if no one's allowed to have fires you can put out, is there? I bet they'd love to come down the Street on Bonfire Night to put 'em out, like they did last year. I know I would if I was a fireman," grumbled Jimmy.

"Penny for the Guy," yelled Terry to a passing punter, and he held out Mr. Barton's old flat cap which was otherwise employed on the Guy's stocking–topped head. The punter coughed up a penny and received a polite thank you in return. Jimmy's dad had told him that 'Guying' was fine provided he did not pester people and was polite, and that he did not start on August Bank Holiday Monday. He had also advised him that, in his personal experience, people preferred to see a regular pitch set up for the five or six days before Bonfire Night, and that familiarity bred generosity. Although Mrs. Barton did not approve of begging, she conceded her husband's point that a well made Guy could be considered as a form of artistic endeavour and worthy of a reward. Terry and Jimmy's Guy however was pitiful, but the sight of the three miserable looking urchins huddled on the cold pavement drew the pennies in. The boys were miserable because there was not going to be a bonfire this year, and the Guy was miserable because, bonfire or not, he knew that he was destined for the flames. They stuck to their pitch right through the rush hours and were hard pressed to make their presence known when the 38s and 73s arrived in quick succession. Mr. Doolan grunted at them when they asked for a penny, and he disappeared into the Half Moon. Being Irish and Catholic, he probably approved of poor old Guido Fawkes, and intended to drink to his health.

Terry and Jimmy split their earnings and got up off their haunches when the stream of homecoming workers had dried up.

It's bleedin' perishing," said Jimmy.

"Yeah. I'm gonna get a bag of chips," said Terry, and they joined the queue in the hot steamy chip shop.

By the time Terry had been served Jimmy had decided to forego the pleasures of three more bangers by spending some of his firework money on a bag of chips as well.

"Could I have some crackling with it?" He said to the man who was serving him.

"Sure son," the man smiled and looked at the drooping Guy under Jimmy's arm, "And what's your mate having? He looks like he could do with warming up a bit."

The Guy winced and the chip shop queue laughed. Jimmy and Terry escorted the embarrassed Guy down to the Cornwall Gate where they sat on the steps and ate their chips.

The next morning Jimmy answered a knock on the front door. His mum had just left to go to work and he was contemplating taking a trip down to Buddings to buy more fireworks with his 'Guying' money.

"Are you coming out Jim?"

Alan was leaning against the railings of the balcony.

"Yeah," said Jimmy as he stepped back inside to fetch his jacket.

They walked past Mrs. Smith's flat at the top of the stairs and went down one flight to the second balcony.

"Let's see if Terry's in," said Jimmy.

They ran along the balcony, past the flat where Alan lived with his mum, his dad and his little sister, and into the dark dead–end spur where Terry lived, and almost collided with his Nan. She reassured them that Terry was up and about. They watched her slowly walk on swollen legs towards the staircase while they waited for Terry to find his key, as his Nan would be out shopping all morning with his mum.

"Fancy going down the Bottom to get some fireworks?" Jimmy's money was burning a hole in his pocket.

"Yeah, I reckon. We can have a look over the ruins on the way," said Terry.

Alan's agreement to these plans was taken for granted as he was a year younger than the other two. They went out of the Gate to the corner of Quinn Buildings where they abutted the bomb ruins.

"It's gone alright," said Alan as he stared at the empty thousand square yards of arid ground in the middle of which used to stand the focus of Bonfire Night, "No bonfire tomorrow then."

The three boys turned disconsolately away and went down to Buddings to cheer themselves up.

With sore tongues from too many 'Acid Drop Spangles', and with pockets full of fireworks, Jimmy, Terry and Alan strolled up the Street on their way back from Buddings. They were going to spend the afternoon playing cards in Jimmy's front room. As they came opposite the Queens' Gate Alan put his hand up to shield his mouth and whispered, "Ain't that Raymond over there?"

They stopped walking.

"Where?"

"Over the ruins. There, in Britannia Row," Alan said without pointing.

"Open yer eyes Jim, he's over there!" said Terry trying not to point, and exasperated at Jimmy who was more concerned for the fireworks in his bulging pockets, which he wanted to get safely stashed away under his bed.

"He's just gone round by the church hall. Look."

"What's he up to?" said Jimmy, fearful for his fireworks.

Suddenly Raymond reappeared, followed by some of his mates who were carrying old floor boards and joists which they dumped under what used to be the party wall of the church hall, and was now next to the ruins. They heard Raymond shout out something, and they followed his gaze upward to the roof parapet of the three–storey building. It was then that they noticed a large pulley, attached to a couple of scaffold poles, protruding from the parapet.

"I've never noticed that wheel up there before," said Alan.

"It's a pulley, stupid." said Terry.

The upper torsos of two young men suddenly appeared next to the scaffold poles, and one lad threw down a rope, which the boys could now see was running free on the pulley. The other young man pushed a large bucket, which was attached to the other end of the rope, over the parapet and lowered it down to the waiting Raymond.

"That's Peter Sullivan up there, ain't it?" said Terry.

"How'd he get up there?" said Jimmy.

"Look, Ray's putting those planks of wood into that bucket," said Alan open mouthed.

Raymond was supervising the up ending of joists and planks into the cement–encrusted bucket. He then tied their loose ends tightly to the pulley rope, and he and his team hauled on the free end of the rope. The bucket jerked its way up the rendered wall of the Church Hall.

"They ain't gonna have a bonfire up there are they?" said Alan

"No, stupid. I reckon they're gonna hide all that wood on the roof," said Terry.

The planks and joists had reached the pulley and Peter Sullivan untied them and leaned them on the edge of the parapet. The bucket was hauled up a little further and three pairs of hands eased the wood over the parapet and on to the roof. Only one short plank fell back down, but sensibly the boys below were standing well out of the way. The bucket was returned to the ruins and while it was being loaded again, Peter and Raymond were giving and getting instructions, and Peter was pointing towards the Queens' Gate.

"Is he pointing at us?" said Alan.

"I bloody hope not," said Jimmy, but Raymond was beckoning at them to come over.

"We'd better see what he wants," said Terry.

"Oh shit," said Jimmy and he kept half a pace behind the others as they crossed the Street and walked on to the bomb ruins, where Raymond met them half way.

"What's going on Ray?" asked Terry.

"What's it look like?" said Raymond, "Those bastards ain't gonna stop us having a bonfire. Peter Sullivan wants you three to keep a look out while we get this stuff on the roof."

"Yeah, sure Ray, we can do that," said Terry looking at Alan and Jimmy who nodded in agreement; they had no intention of crossing Raymond let alone Peter Sullivan.

Jimmy was relieved that his fireworks lay undiscovered in his pockets as he ran up towards the Cornwall Gate. His job was to look out for any policemen or suspicious vehicles coming down the Street from Essex Road. Alan was posted at the bottom of the Street near the Albany Gate with the same instructions, and Terry was to stand at the Queens' Gate looking out for signals from the other two. He could immediately pass any signals to Raymond on the ruins. Two more lookouts from among Raymond's gang had already been posted at both ends of Britannia Row. When he reached the Cornwall Gate, Jimmy dashed upstairs. He ran around the top balcony, got the front door key out of the scullery window, dumped his fireworks on his bed, hung the key up again and was back in the Gate waving at Terry before his friend had time to panic at his disappearance.

Jimmy had been on sentry duty for half an hour, stamping up and down the pavement outside Mrs. Doolan's bedroom windows to keep warm, when he saw Terry cross over to the ruins. He soon returned, and gesticulated to Jimmy and Alan who ran to rejoin him.

"They've gone to get more wood," said Terry.

"Where're they getting it from?" asked Jimmy.

"Ray wouldn't tell me. He says to wait here until they come back."

"S'pose we'd better then," said Jimmy.

So they played on the ruins and let off a few bangers under tin cans, under little piles of stones and in puddles, until Raymond's gang returned an hour later with a cartload of wood.

"Any sign of The Old Bill?" asked Raymond.

"Nah," said Terry.

"You'd better keep a good look out then."

So they went back to their positions and more and more wooden lumber was raised on to the flat roof of St. James' Church Hall.

The operation was on and off all that afternoon, and also the following day, the 5th of November itself. Only once did the cry go up, 'Coppers', and evidence of the bonfire team's clandestine activities was hastily hidden from the eyes of the lone Bobby who came down the Street on his pushbike.

"Alright lad?" said the policeman to Terry who stood whistling in the Queens' Gate.

Things seemed to be remarkably quiet on this part of his beat for a half term holiday.

"Where are your mates then?"

"Dunno," said Terry.

The policeman was a little suspicious. His instructions were to report any bonfire building he came across taking place on public property. He looked towards the ruins, which strictly speaking were private property, but nobody took any notice of that. He could see no signs of pyrotechnic activity, so he peddled down the Street and past the Albany Gate, which Alan had abandoned a moment before. From his crouched position behind the roof parapet of the Church Hall, Peter Sullivan watched the policeman disappear, and then he signalled the all–clear to Raymond who was waiting below, out of sight in Britannia Row. Work was resumed, and Terry, Alan and Jimmy jumped up and down and waved to each other in triumph.

As word got around concerning the hoard of wood on the Church Hall roof, many kids volunteered for lookout duties and became part of the great bonfire conspiracy, and everybody else became an accessory after the fact.

Peter Sullivan had seen his reputation threatened by the removal of the original bonfire by the Fire Brigade, and he had taken time off sick from his job as an apprentice scaffolder, to sort things out. He had liberated some scaffold poles, a builders' hoist and a cart from his employers' yard, and had used his contacts in the trade to locate discarded timber from demolition jobs. Together with some members of his gang from Quinn Buildings, he had come up with the idea of storing the stuff temporarily out of sight on the roof of the Church Hall. Fortunately the unsuspecting caretaker of the hall was the unfortunate father of one of the gang and his keys had been copied. As dusk settled on Friday afternoon, and Bonfire Night began, the last bucket–load of old roof battens was hoisted up to the roof. The conspirators dispersed, but only to return a couple of hours later.

Jimmy was at home when his mum came in from work.

"What time are you going out Jimmy?" she asked.

"After tea mum, I'm knocking for Terry and we're going over the ruins to see the bonfire."

"I thought the firemen had cleared it all away."

"They've got another load of stuff to burn now," said Jimmy.

"I didn't see anything when I came up the Street just now."

"It's all on the Church Hall roof mum."

"Well I never," she said as she stepped over Jimmy's fireworks that were lined up in a long row on the floor of the front room.

"You'll have to clear this lot away before someone slips arse over head."

Jimmy placed his individually selected and now intimately known and slightly grubby fireworks into the biscuit tin, and took them into the bedroom to join the half crown box of 'Astra' fireworks that his mum had bought him the day before. He went back to the scullery and told his mum all about what he had been doing during the last two days.

"Well I never," she said for the umpteenth time, "I knew nothing about it."

In fact it was only at the end of that afternoon that the vicar of St. James' found out about it from his horrified caretaker. By the time he got around to visiting the Church Hall, Peter Sullivan's gang was throwing all kinds of old timbers off the roof and on to the ruins below. It was too late to protest, and the vicar thought it best to let the boys clear the stuff off his building. So he watched from the safety of Britannia Row with a small crowd of people that was slowly gathering.

Jimmy went out and stood on the balcony. He looked across the Square to the flats opposite, and above the rooftops he could see rockets exploding in the distance, forming a sparse and uncoordinated pattern in the darkening sky. Down in the Cornwall Square small groups of people were setting off fireworks and waving sparklers, and little kids were being initiated into the rites of Guy Fawkes Night. A few families were doing the same from the balconies. Roman candles tied to stanchions were sending sparks arcing down into the Square, and a couple of rockets wooshed out of milk bottles angled between the railings. There was no flickering orange glow above the roofs in the direction of the ruins, so Jimmy knew that the bonfire had not yet been lit. He ran excitedly down the stairs and waved to Alan who was setting off fireworks with his father outside their front room window. The faces of his mum and his little sister were lit up on the other side of the glass.

"Hey, Alan, are you coming over the ruins later on?" Jimmy called out.

Alan looked at his father and then called back an OK. Alan's dad was strict with his son, and even Jimmy was afraid of him.

"My dad thinks your mum and dad spoil you," Alan had once said to Jimmy, and of course it was true.

Terry was just finishing his tea when Jimmy knocked for him.

"Nan, I'm going over the ruins with Jimmy to see the bonfire," Terry shouted up the passage as he shut the front door.

"Did you let your fireworks off then?" asked Jimmy.

"Yeah, me and Barbie were down in the Square outside me mum's half an hour ago, didn't you see us?" said Terry whose little half sister Barbara was just old enough to appreciate a firework show.

"No, I must've been having me tea," said Jimmy, "I've still got all my fireworks upstairs. I'm gonna set 'em off later."

He wanted to get the maximum pleasure out of his fireworks, when there were fewer distractions around and less competition from other displays.

They walked down to the Square, waved at Alan and then dashed through the Gate to join the crowd on the edge of the ruins, which were not safe to cross yet as timber was still being thrown down from the Church Hall roof. When Peter Sullivan announced that the last split scaffolding plank was on its way down, a gang of willing bonfire builders ran on to the ruins and soon a fifteen foot conical structure surrounded by expectant children was standing in the middle of the ruins. Someone in the Sullivan gang, it might have been Raymond, poured a gallon of petrol over the timbers and Peter set the bonfire alight. The crowd on the ruins cheered as the blaze took hold, and a few kids came up close to throw their Guys on to the flames.

"I've forgotten the Guy," said Jimmy to Terry, and he ran back to his flat to fetch it.

Jimmy's dad had just got home from work.

"What's up Jimmy, you got a squib up your arse?"

"I've got to put the Guy on the bonfire dad, I forgot all about it."

"You can always use it again next year. Can't he Martha?"

"I'm not having that dirty thing in here for a year," said Mrs. Barton, "I'll be glad to see the back of it. It gives me a fright every time I go in the bedroom, and there it is glaring at me from the top of the wardrobe."

So the Guy did not get a reprieve, and Jimmy took it over the ruins. He met Alan on the way down the stairs and they soon found Terry in the crowd around the bonfire. Terry unceremoniously tossed the Guy into the flames and Jimmy shivered involuntarily. He had become rather attached to their creation, and he was just a bit anal–retentive. The paper stuffed figure shrivelled up into nothing, but Mr. Barton's old flat cap was drawn into the hot gaseous stream above the bonfire, where it burst into flames and fell smouldering at their feet.

"Let's go and find the others," said Alan, and the three boys searched the faces lit up by the bonfire, dodging the sparking bangers, the unpredictable jumping Jacks, and the squibs which raced around the ruins causing people to leap around in a demented fashion. They delved into their pockets for their bangers, and joined in the whiz–bang going on all around them. They found Barry, Mike and Steve further down the ruins beyond the Queens' Gate where they were engaged in an orgy of banger throwing.

Having exhausted their supplies of bangers and jumping Jacks the six boys, with inane grins on their faces, then wandered among the groups of people setting off fireworks on the ruins. They stopped to watch rockets go up and snowstorms to subside, and stepped in to assist where fireworks failed to ignite, and they spluttered in the smoke from hundreds of spent fireworks. The dying fire glowed orangely in the drifting incandescent smoke, and gradually the silhouettes and ghostly figures of Cottagers began to drift away with it. Jimmy announced that he was now going to let off his fireworks, and as his friends had already disposed of theirs, they followed him to the Cornwall Gate. Guy Fawkes Night was not yet over.

The Square was empty of people but a few sparklers and coloured fountains were still giving pleasure around the balconies. Jimmy drew his friends into the passage of his flat and went into the bedroom to fetch his fireworks. Mr. Barton opened the back room door.

"Watch'ya lads, cold enough for you?" he said, "Where is he?"

"Getting his fireworks," said Terry, "He must be the last one around here with any left."

Jimmy emerged with his biscuit tin and his box of 'Astra' fireworks.

"He's been saving those up for weeks," said Mr. Barton.

Jimmy opened his box for one last look, and then he announced in a cracked voice that he did not want to let them off.

"What do you mean Jimmy, that's what you bought them for didn't you? You and the boys take them down in the Square and enjoy yourselves."

"But they're mine. And everyone else will see them going off, and when they've all gone there won't be any more until next year," Jimmy snivelled, and he thought that life was very unfair.

"Come on Jimmy. Don't show yourself up," said his dad, "These are all your friends here, ain't they? Go and set 'em off, you've been looking forward to this for weeks."

Everyone stared at Jimmy who was battling with a surfeit of emotion and exhilaration that had been building up all week.

"It's now or never son, these things aren't made to last," said Mr. Barton and he put his arm around Jimmy and took him on to the balcony, preceded by his friends.

Above the rooftops there was still a faint glow from the residue of the bonfire, and a few straggly rockets made insubstantial trails in the smoke filled North London sky. Jimmy grew less agitated. Guy Fawkes Night had come and it had almost gone, and for Jimmy it was nearly too late to play his part in it.

"Let's get a move on then," he said, and a subdued string of boys followed him along the balcony.

At the top of the stairs Jimmy heard his name called and he turned to see Mrs. Smith standing in her doorway. He went over to her while his friends shuffled their feet nearby.

"Oh, hello Mrs. Smith, we're just going down to set off my fireworks now, before everybody's gone home," said Jimmy.

"I'm glad I caught you," she said, "Wait here a minute," and she disappeared into her flat and returned with a five bob box of 'Brocks' fireworks.

"I bought these for my grandchildren. They were coming round this evening for the bonfire, but I expect their dad has been held up. You and the boys had better have these, they're no use to me."

Jimmy looked at his friends and their eyes opened wide and were filled with firework mania.

"Wow, thanks Mrs. Smith," said Jimmy.

"Yeah, thanks a lot," said Terry and Alan, the other Cornwall kids.

Jimmy took the box of fireworks.

"You can watch us set them off in the Square," he said as they started to go down the stairs.

"No, it's alright Jimmy, you go off and enjoy them with your friends," and she shut the door.

Jimmy and the little gang of pyromaniacs, with renewed enthusiasm and expectations, ran through the Airey and into the Square of Queens Cottages. Unlike the other three Squares, this one still contained half of a well–trodden garden retained across the middle by a long wall, against and upon which, the host of fireworks was set off. A couple of late starters were still dodging about the Square and, together with the few Cottagers who came out of their doors to see what the noise was about, made an appreciative audience for the firework display, courtesy of Mrs. Smith and Jimmy.

After the last Roman candle had fired its last green ball above their heads to a final cheer, the boys split up. Barry, Mike and Steve, who all lived in Queens Cottages said "See ya," and drifted away up the stairs. Alan, Terry and Jimmy strolled out of the Gate and crossed the Street, and had a last look at the embers of the bonfire that was not supposed to be. A few kids were still hanging around; collecting spent fireworks and throwing them on to the hot cinders.

Sometimes they were rewarded with a spurt of blue flame, a white magnesium flash, a hiss or a crackle of sparks.

The indescribable smell of spent gunpowder and wood smoke lingered heavily under the inverted November sky. Dew was already settling as Jimmy, Terry and Alan walked up the eerily still Street to their Gate.

"Fancy coming out early tomorrow to look for dud bangers?" said Jimmy enthusiastically, "We can collect the gunpowder and have a laugh setting it off."

"Maybe Jimmy, maybe," said Terry and Alan wearily as they climbed the stairs.

THIS OLD SHIRT OF MINE

Christmas was the third event of the year that Jimmy looked forward to with over–joyous anticipation. In his holiday hit parade Christmas came between the annual trip to the seaside at number one and Guy Fawkes week at number three. Like every other kid he looked forward to getting Christmas presents and to all the members of his family being at home at the same time, but he tended to build his expectations up too high. He expected snow, if not at Christmas then at least in January. He expected to play cards and 'Consequences' for days on end. He hoped that the 'inlaws and the outlaws' as Mr. Barton called them would visit, and he hoped that his friends would want to play out during the cold and dreary weeks of the Christmas school holidays. Even though he was only a kid he already understood that reality and expectation bore very little resemblance to each other, and he tried to compensate for the disappointments of reality by investing heavily in the anticipation of Christmas. It was something he also did in the lead up to the summer holidays and to Guy Fawkes night.

The children of Miss Steifle's class put up the Christmas decorations they had made during the last weeks of the

Autumn term, mostly lots of coloured paper chains laboriously glued together with lumpy London County Council gum, and a half–hearted Christmas party was held in the classroom. It was nowhere near as good as the big magical parties that were held in the hall of Charlie Mutton Infants and where Jimmy had come across lime flavoured jelly for the first time.

Mrs. Barton was a member of the Christmas loan club that operated from the upstairs room of the 'Clothworkers Arms' in Dame Street. The club loaned money to its members at Christmas time and for emergencies, and it also functioned as a savings bank. Either way Jimmy's mum financed the Barton's Christmas from the loan club. It was not unknown for the organisers of Christmas loan clubs to embezzle the funds just before pay out night and ruin a lot of family Christmases, but fortunately this had never happened at Mrs. Barton's club. She went on Monday evenings to the pub and joined the queue on the stairs to pay over her subs, and sometimes Jimmy went with her. He was not allowed inside the 'Clothworkers Arms' but his mum always bought him a packet of Smith's crisps and a bottle of lemonade from the pub's off–licence and he would sit on the kerb outside the pub to wait for her. Jimmy loved crisps but it seemed to him that the only place they were sold was in pubs. His consumption was restricted to the occasional bag on Monday evenings, or when his dad brought some home from the Packington Arms, which he usually forgot to do despite Jimmy's regular reminders.

While he waited for his mum Jimmy passed the time searching the pavement and the gutters near the pub for Crown beer bottle caps even though he knew that he was unlikely to find any. Most beer bottles were either opened inside the pub or in people's homes, and if he did find any they would probably be bent and useless anyway. The brightly coloured metal caps with their sharply crimped edges were prized among the Street kids because they could be used to decorate jumpers and box carts, but they had to be good specimens. In order to decorate a jumper the sliver of cork that lined the inside of the bottle cap had to be prised out in one piece using a penknife. The cap could then be placed on the outside of the jumper and the cork pressed into it from the inside so that it was tightly held in position. Some boys managed to fix scores of multi–coloured bottle caps on to the sleeves and the fronts of their jumpers. Inevitably this process resulted in holes which the Street kids unconvincingly blamed on moths. Fortunately for his mum Jimmy did not have a reliable source of bottle caps and his jumpers remained largely unsullied.

Although he envied boys who could decorate their clothes with bottle caps he was really jealous of those boys who had a pushcart to embellish. The simplest carts were made from a short length of scaffold plank, two pairs of pram wheels, some six inch nails, a length of wood, some string and a nut and bolt. The plank was often festooned with bottle caps nailed through their centres to form patterns or initials, but Jimmy had neither a cart nor a store of bottle caps with which to decorate it. His problem was getting the materials, especially pram wheels, which were at a premium, and also finding tools and the skill to use them. His good friend Terry had acquired a cart at one time but he had made the mistake of letting Jimmy use it. He was racing it downhill on the pavement from the Edinburgh end of the Street, steering with his feet but he brought the cart too close to the wall of the Cottages. The front wheel hub scraped along the hard rendered plinth with such force that the vibrations shook the rubber tyres off the front wheels. They tried to lever them back on using Mrs. Barton's cutlery but the forks and spoons were not up to the job. So Terry looked for a new set of wheels and Jimmy never rode on a cart again, to the relief of the contents of his mum's knife drawer.

Jimmy's mum emerged from the 'Clothworkers Arms' with a group of women he did not know. They were all laughing and clutching bottles of beer and bags of crisps. They had just celebrated the Christmas loan club pay–out with a drink at the bar, something they never did on normal Monday evenings, and by dropping the loan club man a couple of bob by way of a Christmas box.

"Let's get home now Jimmy, your father will be wondering what I've got up to."

She was clutching her purse in one hand and a bottle of Mackeson in the other.

"All set for Christmas now – I'll get you fitted out down at Dawson's on Saturday, and I'll order the joint from Boundy's tomorrow."

"Ain't we going to have a chicken mum?" Jimmy asked anxiously, because chicken was a rare dish at the Barton table and he had never tasted anything quite so good before.

"Yes I'll get you a chicken Jimmy. I'd get a turkey but your father insists on his belly of pork as well, and a turkey would then be far too much for us." They walked back to Cornwall Cottages discussing Christmas dinner.

"You can help me make the cake tomorrow."

Mrs. Barton got most of her shopping in Essex Road. She had no time to go much further afield, except to buy special items such as furniture. But at Christmas time she took Jimmy to Dawson's near Old Street for his annual clothing fit out and to buy curtaining material and one or two Christmas presents. She also made one of her rare trips to Chapel Market at the Angel. The market was cheaper than the Essex Road shops but it was quite a walk with shopping bags, and the bus fares and the precious time taken to get there and back took the edge off any savings she might make. Mr. Barton's three sisters, the ones with the Holy Water and Flo, who did not go out to work, all shopped in Chapel market almost on a daily basis.

"Your Aunt Flo's done her housework by nine and she's on her way to Chap before I've got my apron on at Canda's." Jimmy's mum observed as they rounded the corner into Liverpool Road on a dark December afternoon.

She could not help looking at the jewellery in Sidney Smith's glittering windows that followed the corner around.

"Your dad says he's going to get me another engagement ring. I had to sell the first one years ago to buy your sister's school uniform. But perhaps we should wait and see which school you'll be going to next September Jimmy before we do in our dough."

He was going to take his eleven plus exam in the new year.

"I don't want to go to the big school mum," he whined.

"You'll have to mate. You'll need an education if you don't want to end up like me and your father. We both left school at 14 with nothing but a testimonial – you know, 'trustworthy and willing to work'."

Jimmy could not see what was so bad about being like his mum and dad and living in the Cottages.

"Don't you like it down the Street mum?"

"D'you know what Jimmy. I hate it. I hate living in a flat, the dirt and the bloody neighbours. I'd like my own house with a garden or even a yard. As for Islington Council and the sweaty cloth cap Labourites who run it, they'll never get round to housing people like us. I don't want their bloody charity anyway. You know what I'd really like? A bit of ground. I'd build a house and I could make things grow – anywhere."

And Jimmy believed she could too. She was a natural, stand on your own two feet, boot straps working class Tory Romantic.

"We could emigrate mum."

"Don't be daft. Your father would hate it."

With the growing crowd of shoppers they shuffled past 'The Pied Bull' and turned into Chapel Street where the gutters were lined on both sides with market barrows, and the roadway and pavements were seething with last minute Christmas shoppers. It was cold and wet and Jimmy's ears tingled. His shoes were sodden from the black slush that was augmented with trodden in sawdust and tissue paper. But the electric light bulbs and the big hissing acetylene lamps strung from the overhead booms of the barrows dispelled the winter gloom. Jimmy became intoxicated with Christmas excitement. Barrows piled up with tin toys, turkeys, holly and mistletoe, decorations, cards and Christmas crackers were scattered among the ubiquitous fruit and vegetable stalls. Others did a hilarious trade in saucy nighties. The two ice cream parlours half way down the street were bursting. Manze's pie shop was still serving up pies and stewed eels. It was full of mums with wide–eyed kids peering between the giant vinegar bottles on the marble–topped tables. The man selling deep fried apple fritters had run out of flour, but the old man with no teeth who sold Percy Dalton's peanuts from a tray was still calling out 'Juts, juts', it was all Jimmy had ever heard him say. A blind accordion player stood under a gas lamp surrounded by squashed fruit, cauliflower leaves and corrugated cardboard, and his collection box was filling up nicely.

Mrs. Barton fought her way to a stall selling bargain boxes of Christmas crackers. The crepe paper bound bundles of mystery that Jimmy rated second only to fireworks were displayed in their holly decorated cardboard boxes – red, green, blue and yellow bon–bons all in rows, each containing a plastic marvel and with a Georgian lady stuck on the front. In answer to Mrs. Barton's question the stallholder confirmed to Jimmy's satisfaction that each cracker was guaranteed to give a sufficiently loud bang. She hurried off to buy holly, tangerines, Spanish nuts and boxes of dates, Turkish delight and 'Black Magic' chocolates, dragging Jimmy along behind her, and he was still clutching the box of crackers tightly under his arm when they got home.

Charlie Barton, pub pianist, was in great demand at Christmas time. On whatever days of the week they occurred he always played in the Packington Arms on Christmas Eve, Christmas Day and Boxing Day. This sometimes meant that he was playing on five or six consecutive nights if a weekend was tacked on. The Christmas Eve and Boxing Day sessions were the longest and most lucrative for Mr. Barton, and he enjoyed himself greatly. Martha Barton refused most of his invitations to come down the pub with him; she was far too busy. But on Christmas Day the pubs kept to Sunday opening times and Mr. Barton was at home for most of the day.

Indeed Christmas Day was very much like a glorified Sunday. Jimmy usually spent the time leading up to Christmas dinner reading the latest Beano and Dandy Annuals and delving into his new children's encyclopaedia to find amazing facts with which to astound his friends, and playing with the toys and games he had acquired that morning. Mrs. Barton had got up early to prepare herself for the supreme effort that Christmas dinner entailed. Her exertions were fuelled by an occasional glass of Harvey's Bristol Cream lovingly brought in to the scullery for her by Mr. Barton.

Charlie Barton made his escape to the pub by way of his sisters–of–the–Holy–Water and he left them with a Christmas box. Jimmy's girl cousins turned up in their Christmas best and their Aunt Martha gave them a Christmas box as well.

When they had gone Jimmy gazed into the empty Square and wondered why nobody ever played out on Christmas Day, or on Boxing Day come to that. Sally was round Tommy Wilson's flat in Queens Cottages and there was nothing worth listening to on the radio. There was just an interminably long

and excruciating Christmas edition of Family Favourites
with each terrible song being accompanied by long lists of
people extending seasonal greetings to each other across the
Commonwealth. At least Mrs. Barton was happily singing
in the scullery, "Oh the pot that she piddled in she cooked
her potatoes in...."

Jimmy was relieved when his dad and his sister came
home and dinner was served up. Now they could pull the
crackers and play cards and 'Consequences' until teatime
at least.

Jimmy's mum and dad might drink a glass or two of
beer with their Christmas dinner but very little alcohol was
taken in the Barton household at Christmas or at any other
time. However there was always a bottle of Port and one of
Sherry and perhaps a bottle of gin available but these would
probably still be around a year later, depleted only by a few
well deserved Sunday treats and by an occasional guest.
Charlie Barton did not like having too much drink in the
house, especially spirits as he reckoned that it attracted too
many unwelcome visitors. For a man who spent so much of
his free time in the pub Mr. Barton was surprisingly sober
and he came home after each piano playing session in an
excellent mood after a few brown and milds. Jimmy had
only seen him drunk once and that had nothing to do with
the Packington Arms.

*

On the last working day before Christmas Charlie
Barton was late getting home.

"Where's he got to?" said Mrs. Barton to her son and
daughter, "He said he wouldn't stay long after work. He's
never been this late before."

"He's probably on his way mum. He'll be alright," said
Sally.

"His mate Ronnie, that NATSOPA bloke, can really knock 'em back. Your father's not used to that sort of drinking Sally, he'll get him on to shorts."

"Don't worry mum, he'll be home soon," and she was right.

They heard the key in the door, but there was no little whoop or whistle as Charlie Barton walked up the passage. He opened the door of the front room and hung on to the doorknob drooping slightly.

"You all right Charles?" said Mrs. Barton and she gave him an old fashioned look.

He nodded.

"Where've you been, it's ever so late....and what's up with your face?"

"I've walked from Kings Cross," he spluttered.

Martha gave a gasp and a little cry and Sally stood up quickly.

"What is it mum?"

Charlie Barton stared uncomprehendingly at his wife.

"Charlie. Where's your bottom set?"

He raised an unsteady hand to his jaw.

"You do look a bit weird dad," said Jimmy.

"Oh," said Mr. Barton, and he turned around and made slowly for the front door closely followed by his family.

"Where're you off to now?" demanded Mrs. Barton.

"Kings Cross," he muttered.

"Do you want me to come with you?" she said as he clung to the railings. He shook his head and set off slowly and deliberately around the balcony. The sober members of the family reconvened in the front room.

"He won't be able to enjoy his Christmas dinner without his bottom teeth. Silly man," Mrs. Barton said to no one in particular. Sally looked at her mother and they both grinned.

"It's a serious matter," she could not help smiling, "losing your teeth at Kings Cross."

"Poor dad," said Sally.

An hour and a half later he walked back into the front room again, more steady on his feet this time and his cheeks and bottom lip fully supported in their more familiar positions.

"Thank God," Martha Barton exclaimed, "you found them alright then."

"They weren't lost," he said "I remembered exactly where I'd been sick, an alley near the station, and there they still were, grinning up at me. So I picked 'em up and clamped 'em in...."

"Charlie. You didn't?"

"No. Of course not," he grinned, "I took 'em into the Gents and rinsed 'em under the tap, and then I clamped 'em in."

"What were you doing at Kings Cross anyway?" she scolded.

"Well I got on the Tube at Kentish Town as usual but I felt so ill on the train that I got off again after a couple of stops and walked the rest of the way home. I'm sorry to have worried you Martha. That bleedin' Ronnie kept getting whiskeys in and I sort of lost track of the time."

"You didn't walk back to Kings Cross as well did you?"

"I did. I was still feeling queasy. But once I'd clamped me Hampsteads in I felt like me old self, and I got a 73 bus home. Next time I'll put a double sprinkling of Dr. Wernett's Powder on both sets, that'll keep 'em in."

"What next time?" queried Martha Barton.

"No next time dear. Never again. What's for tea?"

*

Jimmy Barton took his eleven plus examination a month or so after the Christmas holidays. His sister and her fiancé Tommy had both gone to grammar school, Dame Alice Owens at the Angel, and had matriculated, whatever that meant; and his mum and dad would have been pleased if he did the same, but they did not put any pressure on him, none at all. Sally had been coaching him a little in English grammar and Tommy Wilson had given him sums to do but his main encouragement came from Miss Steifle, his teacher at Charlie Mutton Junior Mixed. He regularly came within the top five in class and she had recognised him as a hopeful candidate for passing this greatly divisive examination. Charlie Mutton's record was in the region of a 90% failure rate, and most Old Muttonians finished their education at Queen's Head Street School, the local Secondary Modern. Jimmy was only vaguely aware of the effect that the result of this examination would have on the future direction of his life. If he thought about his adult life at all he saw himself as a craftsman of some kind, perhaps a joiner, even though he showed no aptitude for practical tasks. However he did not fancy spending four years at Queen's Head Street with the local bullies. He liked the sound of Barnsbury Boys School, even though he had no idea where it was.

Barnsbury was a compromise 'Central' school, giving bright working class kids who had failed the eleven plus a chance to become office fodder rather than factory fodder. His friend Terry was determined to go to Barnsbury, it was the school to which most of the pupils of William Tyndale School aspired. If Jimmy went there as well, he and Terry could be best mates in school as well as in the Cottages. So Jimmy was not too concerned about the examination, he just wanted to do well enough to get to Barnsbury with Terry.

Jimmy's examination was held in Miss Steifle's classroom. She did her best to keep the candidates far enough apart to discourage cheating and disruptive intercourse, but with a complement of forty, even with some pupils absent this was not easily accomplished. She gave up her chair and desk for Jimmy to use, and he felt rather conspicuous facing the class as well as embarrassed by what seemed to be Miss Steifle's special attention. But once he got stuck into the tests his self–consciousness left him. As he worked through the test paper he quickly realised that some of the IQ questions were harder than others. So he searched out the easiest to do first and left the more difficult ones to the end. He did not complete all of the questions but Miss Steifle said that this was quite normal. The final part of the examination was a written composition. Jimmy's writing was undisciplined, his spelling had improved, but his knowledge of grammar was rudimentary and his imagination would often run away with him giving rise to a stream of unpolished sentences. Nevertheless Miss Steifle saw English Composition as his most promising subject and was pleased but also concerned to see him busily writing as she declared the examination over. Jimmy was still writing when she began to collect up the papers. She took her time and quite deliberately left Jimmy until last. He was still scribbling frantically when she whipped the papers away from him.

Jimmy Barton was one of five boys and one girl in Miss Steifle's class who passed the eleven plus examination that year. He was pleased with his success even though it meant that he would have to completely overhaul his own expectations. His family and the neighbours thought that he ought to go to a local grammar school and like all upstanding working class folk they never questioned the advice of teachers or those in authority. It was unthinkable now for Jimmy to go to Barnsbury Boys with Terry. Instead he became one of the few Cottage kids to go to grammar school, but of course this would not change him, he would still be a Street kid, or so he expected. Mrs. Page next door bought Jimmy two novels by Dickens by way of congratulations but it took him over 35 years to get around to reading them.

One of the boys from his class who also passed the eleven plus lived in the next block up, Edinburgh Cottages, but Jimmy hardly knew him. Brian Peter's success had been quite a surprise, to himself as much as to the school, because his abilities had never shone through his anti–authority tendencies before. He was the youngest of four children and his mother was rather put out by the extra expense that his passing for grammar school would put her to. However Brian, together with Jimmy and two of the other successful boys from Miss Steifle's class, went for interviews at the same grammar school. Jimmy could have tried for Owens but he decided to join the others and go for Highbury County School instead, another establishment of which, until then, he had been completely unaware. It was situated on the other side of Highbury Corner and was a little further away than Owens but in the opposite direction.

*

Martha Barton took Jimmy for his interview with Mr. Bishop the headmaster at Highbury. With the exception of Zorro Mr. Bishop was only the second man Jimmy had ever seen wearing a black cloak; the first was the tall, cadaverous and severe looking teacher who had escorted them up from the school library to the headmaster's office.

"Thank you Mr. Boston," said Mr. Bishop as he stood up to shake the hand of Jimmy's mum who was a little flustered by this. He explained that Mr. Boston, his deputy, was the Latin master (known to the Canonburian boys, but not to the head, as 'Magister Bostonus') and that he himself taught Civics to the new first year scholars partly as a way of getting to know them. Jimmy had heard of Latin before but he had no idea what Civics were, and he was also highly suspicious of something called Physics which he hoped was not connected with the frightful gymnasium that he and his mother had seen during the earlier conducted tour of the school. Mr. Bishop was a small and thin middle aged man and only slightly taller than Jimmy who had sprung up during his last year at Charlie Mutton's, and had put on some unhealthy pounds as well.

"Hmm.... long trousers I see. Normally the school would expect first year pupils to wear short trousers but I can see that in your case, being a tallish chap, you might feel a little ridiculous in them," he laughed. "I think we can make an exception in your case."

Jimmy was glad that this possibly embarrassing problem had been resolved the instant he knew of its existence.

"He's been wearing long trousers for almost a year now Mr. Bishop, they're his second pair. I can't keep up with his legs," his mother laughed.

Mr. Bishop smiled.

"Of course the other dress rules have to be obeyed by everyone. The school uniform must be worn at all times in school, and on the way to and from school." He paused.

"Well I think that's all he needs to know for the moment about the school rules. However I must have your undertaking Mrs. Barton that if we accept James into our community he will remain with us until he is sixteen and hopefully for longer. We encourage all our boys to take the Ordinary Level examinations after five years and many move on to advanced study in our flourishing sixth form."

Mrs. Barton assured the headmaster that Jimmy would not be taken out of school at the age of 15 to get a job, not while she had anything to do with it.

"We have had a very good report about you from Miss Steifle who informs me that you enjoy writing stories and reading. We have a very fine library – of course you have seen it – and we encourage all the boys to study there and to borrow the books."

"Jimmy regularly borrows books from the public library," Mrs. Barton said, "We go together sometimes."

"And what are you reading currently?" Mr Bishop peered at Jimmy over the top of his glasses.

Jimmy stammered "Well sir, er, I've, er, been reading books about the 'Lost Planet', and, er, I read, er, Mr. Midshipman Easy last term, and er...."

"What about those Jennings books you've been reading Jimmy?" Mrs. Barton turned to the headmaster. "He's been giggling all week over one of them." Jimmy turned slightly red and Mr. Bishop smiled.

"So, you enjoy stories about school life. Well let us hope that you enjoy your school life with us just as much. Of course Highbury County is not a boarding school, so you will not have the same opportunities that Master John Jennings had to get into mishaps."

He smiled again and looked at Jimmy as if he was Bromwich Major, the 'ozard oik' himself.

Jimmy was imbued with the ethos of Linbury Court School, he could even empathise with the two upper class and privileged heroes, Jennings and Darbishire, whose adventures always ended in a terrible 'bish' but which coincidence and good fortune managed to put right. Yet he was perceptive enough to realise that Highbury County School was not going to be a place where 'silly little boys' would be indulged for long, if at all. He was only half aware of his own class position, and it was many years later that the full absurdity of being plucked out of Cornwall Cottages and selected for special middle class training in a pseudo–public school educational system, finally dawned on him.

At the end of the interview Mr. Bishop said that information about the school was now available in the library for distribution and mother and son were ushered downstairs. Mrs. Barton was given a list of clothing that Jimmy was expected to have for the coming September, together with a copy of the school rules. They sat next to Brian Peters and Mrs. Peters who, with several other boys and their parents, were still waiting to be interviewed.

"Hi Brian," said Jimmy.

"Watchya Jim," said Brian.

"We're in the same class at Charlie Mutton's mum."

Mrs. Barton introduced herself to Brian's mother whom she knew by sight from their passing each other in the Street.

"Have you seen the price of all the clothes they're supposed to have?" said Mrs. Peters, "The bleedin' blazer's over three pounds, and there's all this gym stuff – Brian's just added it up – how much is it Brian?"

"Just over nine quid mum."

"How're we supposed to afford that lot, it's gotta be worth more than a week of the old man's wages? And have you seen this note at the bottom? He's not staying at school 'til he's 16. He'll be starting work on his fifteenth birthday just like his brothers did."

"Needs must," said Jimmy's mum who thought that to take a place at the school and not to take full advantage of it was denying the opportunity to another bright boy who would, but she did not point this out to Mrs. Peters.

Jimmy and his mother said goodbye and made their way to the school entrance. In the library he had been quietly reading the school rules and now he felt decidedly queasy as he thought about the fact that 'Games and gymnastics are compulsory....' and 'A shower/bath is compulsory after games'. He really had nothing at all in common with John Jennings.

*

That summer there was no annual holiday at the seaside for Jimmy and his mum and dad. It was a momentous and expensive year for the family, not just because Jimmy started at the big school, but because Sally Barton and Tommy Wilson got married. Jimmy passed through the school holidays in a dream, but also in some trepidation about the coming September when he would become a first year, a 'weed', a nonentity at Highbury County School. However his concerns were completely overwhelmed by the whirlwind of preparations for the September wedding that engulfed the little flat in Cornwall Cottages, which for Jimmy was no bad thing because it stopped him brooding. Of course he had little to do with all the rigmarole, he just had to keep his head down.

The first Saturday in September was warm and sunny. Charlie Barton and his daughter walked arm in arm along the top balcony of Cornwall Cottages. He wore his best suit, freshly dry–cleaned, and a white carnation and she wore a below the knee white wedding dress and veil. Several neighbours came out to wish her well and others looked on from across the Square. Some could not resist throwing confetti. They carefully went down the three flights of stairs to the Gate, slowing slightly at those concrete treads which everybody knew rocked disconcertingly when stepped on. A small group of Cottagers stood in the Gate and watched the couple get into a big black limousine that took them down the Street and around the corner to St. James' church in Prebend Street.

It was the first time that Jimmy had ever sat inside a church with his mum and dad and he did not feel entirely comfortable about it. They had never spoken to him about religion and he supposed that it was something for which they had no need. After the service and the signing of the marriage register photographs were taken on the pavement in front of the church. Jimmy and Tommy's youngest brother Raymond got under the photographer's feet trying to take their own photographs, Jimmy on his Brownie 1 box camera and Raymond on his Kodak 127. Finally the photographer succeeded in lining up the whole congregation, some 50 people, for a group photograph after which most of them made their way to Beale's Restaurant in Holloway Road for the reception, followed by a party in a room over a pub – where else but the Packington Arms. Sally was the eldest among twenty or so cousins, the children of Mr. and Mrs. Barton's siblings, and she was the first of them to get married. The reception and party that followed were to be repeated many times over the coming decades.

Jimmy had not been to such a big family gathering before and he was exhilarated by it. Although he was a member of a large extended family he had seen very little of his relatives. His mother and father had tended to live their lives in isolation, or so it seemed. Perhaps there had once been recriminations, now suppressed, about past and possibly pre–war events, but it was more likely that they just wanted to remain a private couple after experiencing a very crowded childhood. Charlie Barton's family was a bit stand–offish as his wife would say, but Martha Barton's sisters were far more outward going, and so were most of her brothers–in–law, and Martha's character underwent a metamorphosis when she got together with her five sisters.

The wedding celebration above the Packington Arms was a great success. The six daughters of dour costermonger Jim Franks, kept up an exhausting cacophony of chatter, laughter and singing. They exposed their stocking tops in 'Can–Can' fashion, took the lead in the 'Conga' and the 'Hokey Cokey', and at the same time saw that their children, babies and husbands lacked for nothing. Jimmy's uncles danced and flirted outrageously, in shirt sleeves and braces, and one of them, Uncle Pete, who was married to Martha's sister Betty, took turns with Charlie Barton to play the piano. His playing was a bit more manic and less accurate than Charlie's but he certainly got the party jumping. Even Jimmy began to lose some of his inhibitions to the extent that he paused in his fateful consumption of crisps, of which there seemed to be an unlimited supply, to join in the 'Hokey Cokey' and 'Knees Up Mother Brown'.

Uncle Pete, egged on by his brothers–in–law, and propelled by his innate and now alcohol fuelled extroversion, commenced his party piece. Basically it was a song and dance act known to those who had seen it before as 'This Old Shirt of Mine'. A space quickly cleared around him. His sisters–in–law screamed with laughter and took on expressions of mock admonition as Uncle Pete whirled around and sang –

> "Now this old shirt of mine.
> The inside is quite new,
> But the outside has seen some dirty weather."

By this time he had suggestively pulled his braces from his shoulders and had undone all of his shirt buttons.

> "So I'll cast this shirt aside."
> And he did.
> "And I mean to travel wide.
> Far 'cross the ocean I will wander."

Those who had not seen the act before, and especially those in Charlie Barton's extended family, stared in shocked disbelief at this very loud man, approaching middle age, who was doing a strip tease.

> "Now this old vest of mine.
> The inside is quite new,
> But the outside has seen some dirty weather."

There was uproar as Uncle Pete's vest flew across the room to be rescued by Aunt Betty. It was soon followed by his socks and trousers, but she managed to haul him away, with a great grin on his face, still singing – "Far 'cross the ocean I will wander" – without him exposing more than he should.

The party ended at 11.00 o'clock, pub closing time, and the 'inlaws and the outlaws' went back to Hoxton and the inner suburbs. Sally and Tommy were on their way to Lido de Jesselo for their honeymoon and Jimmy and his mum and dad stayed on to clear up a bit.

"I'll come down with Charlie tomorrow and finish off." Mrs. Barton said to the governor of the Packington Arms.

"I wouldn't hear of it Martha," he said "It's been a pleasure seeing you again. You ought to come down more often with the old man."

Maybe she would and maybe she wouldn't. She had enjoyed the family knees up but she was exhausted. She had pulled out all the stops.

"I couldn't keep this lark up Charlie." She said as the three of them walked home.

Things would never be the same again. Sally and Tommy would set up their home in two rooms near Finsbury Park. The flat in Cornwall Cottages would soon be taken over by a new British Relay television set. Jimmy would finally get the second back room as his very own bedroom, and the front parlour where his sister had slept and done her courting would become the living room. And in a few days time Jimmy would enter the next phase of his life, at Highbury County School. His stomach tightened as he thought of it while nervously fingering the new school tie that his mum had made him wear for his sister's wedding.

"That Pete, he's a right one." Mr. Barton laughed.

"There's no stopping him." Said Mrs. Barton.

"Did you see the look on Rose and Rene's face? I thought they were going to pee themselves. Talk about Holy Water."

And they burst into laughter and then into another chorus.

"So I'll cast this shirt aside...."

END

HISTORICAL AND ARCHITECTURAL NOTES

A. The Development of the Cottages

In 1874 the medical officer for Islington reported that the 25 courts and buildings east of Essex Road between Greenman Street and Britannia Row were insanitary. The area was submitted to the Metropolitan Board of Works under the Artisans' and Labourers' Dwelling Act, 1875, for clearance. The area consisted of artisan's cottages and workshops. It was cleared from 1878 onwards. 1,796 people were displaced from about 250 houses over an area of 5 acres and 3,422 were to be rehoused on the same site, almost twice as many. The five parts of the development site had all been sold to developers by 1884, when building began. The four blocks of 'Cottages' in Popham Street, built for 2,000 tenants, were completed in 1889, and Quinn Buildings opposite for 800 tenants in 1886.

B. Charles Booth's 1897 Survey of the Area

The following is a copy of Charles Booth' notes from his celebrated 'Survey of London' made at the close of the 19th century for the area containing the 'Cottages':–

'26 October 1897 Charles Booth walks with Inspector Mason of the 'N' or Islington Division of the Police in the Popham Street area.'

"Starting from the Essex Road. Join Popham Street. A dark narrow street flanked on either side by buildings marked on map dark blue lined with black. *(These maps, prepared by Booth, indicated the socio–economic standing of the inhabitants.)* On the NW side are the 'Cottages', which are high buildings and flush with the pavement, outwardly like a prison, fronting inwards on a court in the centre of which is a very much fenced in plot of flowers with a gas lamp in the centre itself protected with wire netting to keep the glass from breakage. All round the floors run open passages. Mostly tenanted by labourers 'not of the lowest class' earning 25/– to 30/– per week. The Buildings on the opposite side of the road have a rougher character. The wall fronting on the street is broken by low windows and does not look as forbidding as the 'Cottages' but the tenants are rougher notwithstanding. The buildings are four storied.

"2 large rooms weekly rent 5/6d and 5/–
Single rooms 3/– and 4/–
Extra size room 4/6d
"All rooms with good ranges"

Rules at the Entrance

1. All gambling reported to the Police
2. Hawking prohibited
3. All games stopped by superintendent
4. Tenants only allowed within the gates
5. Disorderly conduct stopped by sup't
6. Wilful destruction prosecuted. Broken windows mended at tenants' expense
7. Landings and staircases to be cleaned by tenants

These buildings were built, Mason said, by the Irish Parnellite MP Quinn. There has been a great alteration for the better since a Committee of Ladies took them in hand. They look light to dark blue, more light than dark. A Miss Mackay was the ruling spirit of the Committee, Mason said, she has been there three years at least, not living in the buildings but constantly about.

In the 'Cottages' was a notice 'No fireworks allowed till Nov 5' and the MABY's has a free registry and library in one of the southern blocks. On the SW side of Popham Street nearer Popham Road are a row of 2 storied cottages "the buildings are generally pretty full but these cottages are never empty" generally held by an old couple at 10/– a week who sublet. "A little house is always a great attraction to the working classes than buildings and a safer investment for speculators."

Popham Road, which runs along the bottom of this poor block, is a little road full of small shops which supply upon credit the wants of the neighbourhood. Butchers, newspaper, oil and general shops. Mason said it would be cheaper to buy at the north end of the road in Essex Road but you would only go there if you had ready money. Costers won't supply up on tick not even if they know their customers. "It's not their system of business." The proof of it was he said that many of the Essex Road costers did live in the neighbouring streets. The Board School is here *(Charlie Mutton's)*. All the children just coming out. All booted. Some rather but none very ragged. Fairly clean faces.

C. Architectural Notes

The Cottages consisted of four groups of flats, four storeys high, that had been noted by the architectural historian Nickolaus Pevsner in his 'Buildings of England' series, as being 'fortress like with turrets, where the interior courtyards had open staircases and galleries'. Built in 1889 they had been designed to accommodate up to 1400 Cottagers by an architect called Worley who apparently believed that a semblance of cottage life could be lived at a density of 750 people to the acre. But the density could be far higher than this due to chronic overcrowding and this put a great strain on the fabric of Mr. Worley's buildings, as did the Luftwaffe and the lack of repairs and investment.

The tenements had been planned as one grand design rather than as four separate blocks (see illustration 1). Mr. Worley had enclosed the 700ft long by 150ft wide site with a virtually continuous four–storey brick wall of flats with holes punched out for windows. He then divided the resulting elongated enclosure into four courtyards by building three pairs of short parallel separating blocks of the same height across it. Between each of these pairs there was a dark narrow canyon, about 25ft wide and known as the 'Airey' (see illustration 8), on one long side of which was a four–foot change of level served by a flight of stairs in one corner.

The intermediate blocks stopped short of the all–encompassing perimeter block and this allowed the access balconies and the ground floor paving to pass between.

However it was only possible to walk from one Square into the next at ground level by way of the Aireys because the balconies were discontinuous. The Street sloped down from the Edinburgh end to the Albany end and Mr. Worley had stepped the site and the perimeter block at each Airey (see illustration 6) and the access balconies (Pevsner's 'galleries' was too grand a description), were separated at each change of level. It would have been difficult and unnecessary to provide stairs to connect them all up. However these upper level disconnections between the blocks made them more secure and allowed them to develop individual character. Subsequent post–war planners, who built high density working class housing estates connected by long and continuous pedestrian rat runs at upper levels, might have learned something from Mr. Worley in this respect.

The courtyards of Edinburgh Cottages near the top of the Street and of Albany Cottages at the bottom were irregular in shape. The 'Square' of Edinburgh was in fact long and narrow. Also, that part of the perimeter block that formed the short upper side of the Edinburgh Square was not at right angles to its neighbours and had been completely rebuilt due to bomb damage. In contrast the 'Square' of Albany Cottages was much larger and was actually L shaped to accommodate an odd piece of the site. Cornwall Cottages had its entrance block at a slight angle to its neighbours so that its 'Square' was a mild trapezium in shape. In fact the only 'Square' that came close to being square belonged to Queens Cottages, and that was rectangular. These differences in the shape of the courtyards made each group of Cottages easily recognisable.

The perimeter block, where it faced the Street, rose straight up from the back edge of the pavement. It contained four arched, two storey high openings, which led through to each of the Squares. These entrances ultimately provided the only access to the front door of every flat in the Cottages.

Above each arch and built out from the main wall on the Street side were two narrow semicircular turrets that gave Mr. Worley's design a definite fortress feel about it. From the 'Gate', as each archway was called, two steel staircases with concrete treads and open risers ran up the sidewalls to the first floor access balcony, which ran across the face of the Gate on this side of the Square. Flights of steps continued up from here in mirrored pairs to serve the other two balconies. Generally a third staircase served the balconies from the side of the Square opposite the Gate.

The concrete access balconies and staircases of the flats were supported by a mixture of circular iron posts and steel I stanchions, the latter being unsympathetic replacements for war damaged round ones. The balcony balustrades consisting of iron railings running between the posts made the balconies completely open to view (See illustration 4).

The dwellings consisted of two basic designs, a two room flat and a three room flat (See illustration 2). Each flat had a small scullery out of which a WC cubicle was partitioned. Each block contained a refuse chute (i.e. 4 to every 'Square') with a small collecting box at ground level. These brick boxes were replaced in the late 1950s by larger enclosures containing tall steel refuse bins, including a separate enclosure built in the middle of each 'Square' for the use of ground floor tenants. Also in the early 1950s some ground floor flats were enlarged and improved with the addition of bathrooms. Electricity was gradually introduced into the flats during the late 1950s.

D. The End of the Cottages

In March 1963, after many years of suffering poor maintenance and money grabbing landlords, the decontrolled tenants of the Cottages sought help from Islington Borough

Council in resisting a proposed rent increase to £3 (an increase of between 133% to 240%). A meeting was held at the South West Islington Labour Party rooms, with sympathetic Councillors chairing. The North London Press (1/3/1963) reported that *'Some tenants... had seen rats and bugs in their flats, damp conditions had impaired their health and sacrifices had been made to find the money to make their homes liveable'*. A tenants association was formed and a committee of 12 was set up with Councillor Arthur Bell as Chairman. On the advice of the Council the tenants successfully resisted paying the full amount of the rent increases.

In December 1963 an angry meeting was held in St James Church Hall, at which, in the presence of 7 Islington Councillors including Arthur Bell, a resolution demanding that the Council compulsory purchase the Cottages was passed. A champion, in the person of Cottager Harry Symons, the Secretary of the Tenants Association, led the Cottage revolt. The angry mood was fuelled by the landlord's demand that new tenants must pay £4 10s and sign what Mr Symons described as 'an impossible and outrageous agreement'. Part of the agreement read: –

"I shall be responsible for the installation of electric lighting to the landlord's satisfaction within a period of four weeks, and shall further be responsible for the maintenance, replacement, repair of all internal fittings, pipes, wiring, fireplaces, windows, sashcords etc. and for any excesses of rates and water rates. I shall undertake to put the flat into suitable decorative condition to the landlord's approval and satisfaction."

Meanwhile the Council had campaigned to improve living conditions at the Cottages. They had served 164 intimation notices and 40 statutory notices on the landlord.

'But', said Mr Symons, as reported in the Islington Gazette (20/12/1963), *'we are not satisfied. The solution to our problems lies in positive action – not pious promises.'*

In January 1964 Islington Council turned down the Tenants' Association's demand for the compulsory purchase of the Cottages.

In March and May 1964 The North London Press reported that the landlord, Fanderfield Investments Ltd, had been prosecuted for non compliance with the notices. But in September the Tenants' Association felt compelled to write to the Council demanding to know why the owners had still not been forced to comply, claiming that officials had *'failed to do their job'* and demanding once again that the flats be compulsory purchased. The Cottagers' champion, Mr Symons, said *'it is the only possible solution to the problem'*. He had also stepped up the campaign by writing to the Leader of the Opposition, Harold Wilson, and to the Minister of Housing, Sir Keith Joseph. The North London Press also quoted the agent for the owners as saying *'We have submitted a selection of draft schemes for improvements to Islington Council and have asked for tenders in connection with these proposals. We propose to alter the position of the wc.s and put in bathrooms. Some of the flats already have bathrooms.'*

The struggle continued for another year or so as Islington Council tried and failed to find the political will to buy out the landlords and indeed to find the money to do so, the latter being by far the greater problem. The landlord procrastinated in carrying out improvements and repairs as the Cottages were now blighted by indecision, although it was doubtful whether these would have been carried out anyway. The buildings were totally unsuited to any realistic programme of upgrading, which, even if carried out in a minimal way, would have been prohibitively expensive. Patch repairs and other holding measures were all that the buildings were worthy of while still in occupation. Their days were long numbered. The landlords realised this but in the meantime they milked the tenants for all that they could. The Council realised this as well but had to go through the motions of issuing repair notices because they could afford to do nothing else. Of course the tenants had quickly come to realise that the Cottages were not viable. They wanted the Council to buy them and to knock them down and to rehouse everybody in Parker Morris splendour.

During this stalemate period two events occurred that were to change the fortunes of the Cottagers and seal the fate of the Cottages. On April 1 1965 the Greater London Council was created, and on March 31 1966 Labour won a landslide victory in the General Election. The sweaty cloth–capped Labourites, as Martha Barton called them, at Islington Council now had sympathetic ears in Westminster and in County Hall. The political will to improve the housing conditions of the Cottagers was bolstered, and slum clearance money was made available.

In June 1966 at a public meeting of the Tenants' Association Harry Symons reported that a resolution had been sent to both Islington Council and the Greater London Council demanding once again that the flats be taken over by Islington. The resolution pointed out that although the flats were not classed as slums *'it is only the hard work and expense on the part of the tenants which have not allowed them to become slums.'* One of the letters read out at the meeting was from Albert Evans, Labour MP for SW Islington. It said that the Islington Town Clerk had said that the GLC and Islington were further considering the future of the flats but that *'to date a final decision has yet to be made. You will appreciate that a matter of such consequence does necessarily take considerable time to debate.' (Islington Gazette 10/6/1966)*

Four months later Islington Council announced that it had paid £200,000 to Fanderfield Investments Ltd for the privilege of knocking down the Popham Street flats. The council had served about 600 notices on the landowners over the previous 4 years to get repairs done but now it was starting *'a new era in its housing redevelopment programme'*. About 1000 people living in overcrowded conditions in the buildings were to be rehoused by 1970–71, the four storey blocks would be demolished and new flats built in their place. At a jubilant meeting at the town hall Alderman Ernest Bayliss, the chairman of Islington's Housing Committee, was cheered when he announced to more than 350 tenants present that they would become council tenants and that they would have the chance of moving to other flats in Islington or to outside towns. Being politically astute he said their homes were not 'slums' but that they were 'sub–standard'. Rents would remain unchanged and tenants who had appealed against recent rent increases would carry on paying their original rent, and the Council would negotiate for the return of any 'key money'. Harry Symons, his job done, resigned at the meeting and received an ovation. He said *'It has taken us three years. But I always expected this and I am not surprised. We have achieved these results without any public demonstrations or marches. We are all very pleased'* (Islington Gazette 7/10/1966). Alderman Bayliss told the North London Press (7/10/1966) *'This purchase in Popham Street represents a further instance of the successful working of the partnership with the GLC to bring all the sub–standard blocks in the borough under local authority control. It will bring to an end these congested ill lit, run down old buildings conceived in the gaslight era.'*

There was one dissenting voice in all the celebration and this came from Islington's 'rebel' councillor, Harry Black, who claimed that the price paid by the council for the Cottages was 'ridiculous'. He said that properties which had been declared slums were bought in the past at site–value. But because these buildings were solidly built and only 'near–slums' the council had to pay £200,000. He said his criticisms were directed at 'the powers that be in Whitehall' for not helping councils to buy 'near–slum' properties. However he congratulated the council on the purchase. Alderman Bayliss said that the price was reasonable considering where the buildings were situated, challenging Mr Black to get his committee *'land at that or a lower price'* (Islington Gazette 14/10/1966).

Three months later in January 1967 the building of six storey, system built flats in an area to the east of Popham Street was announced. The project involved the demolition of several streets of fine old houses. The 540 *'modern centrally heated flats'* designed by Mr Harry Moncrieff, would *'lead on to wide walkways, overlooking traffic free green squares where ... children can play'* (Islington Gazette 6/1/1967). It was to these new Islington Council tenements, known as the Packington Estate, that many Cottagers were destined to be sent. However it would take at least two years for the project to be completed and those Cottagers who could not wait took the opportunity, when offered, of a place in one of Islington's older properties. A year later Charlie and Martha Barton accepted a walk–up flat on the Sickert Estate further along Essex Road. They could not bear to live in the Cottages any more as neighbours and friends moved out and more and more flats were boarded up. Charlie Barton had lived in Cornwall Cottages for the best part of 55 years and he didn't want to stay and watch its slow, depressing demise. It took four years to decant everybody from the Cottages and then the buildings were unceremoniously demolished. Alderman Bayliss had achieved his intention *'to eliminate these sites from the face of Islington'.*

Perhaps it was the natural order of things in a non–egalitarian society that the Essex Road slums of 1874 should have been cleared away to make room for even more overcrowded tenements, the Cottages, that were themselves demolished 100 years later as slums in their own right. The buildings that eventually replaced them were two storey flat roofed terraced houses of a somewhat innovative design, recreating the warrens of cheap housing that had occupied the site prior to the Cottages. Would these dwellings for ordinary working Londoners eventually turn into slums themselves after another 100 years or sooner?

It was during the 1960s that the gentrification of south Islington really got going. The area had many beautiful Georgian, Regency and Victorian terraced houses nearly all of which were in multiple occupation by ordinary working people in virtual slum conditions. The middle classes were starting to return to these houses after an absence of a century or more. Landlords were adding to the housing problems of working people, and therefore of Islington Council, by selling many such houses for the eventual sole occupation of well–off individual families, houses which at one time may have accommodated three families. It was unfortunate that the clearance of the Popham Street slums led indirectly to the demolition of 12 acres of such lovely old houses in the Packington Street area. They would have made excellent investments for the incomers. However it would have been possible to use them to rehouse some of Islington's established residents, including those from Popham Street, in sensitive conversions. The domestic architectural heritage of Islington was under threat from such wholesale demolition and the gentrification process did much to help preserve this heritage but at the long–term expense of a diminishing and increasingly ghettoised working class community.

At the same time that the Cottages of Popham Street were being emptied the local press was full of the debate about the fate of Islington's long abused street architecture, a debate fuelled by the concerns of the newcomers. It was in the glare of this debate that the following letter appeared in the Islington Gazette. It was written by a friend of the author and was one of a series of spoof letters that he wrote, many of which were also published. To this day neither the author nor his friend knows whether or not the Editor published the letters because of their ironic tone or because he thought that a serious point was being made.

17 Jan 1967From "Islington Gazette" letters page

"Regarding the statement (Gazette, Jan 10) that much of Islington's beautiful architecture is to be preserved I feel I must complain about the plan proposed by the council to demolish one of the borough's most picturesque groups of buildings.

I refer, of course, to that charming group of tenement dwellings in Popham Street which are to be pulled down to make way for modern sky–scraper blocks with no character whatsoever.

Being a resident myself, I must inform you that if the plan is allowed to succeed it will wield a bitter blow for many of the tenants.

Filth and squalor breed friendliness and everyone in the buildings knows everyone else.

One has only to walk into any of the squares to be immediately struck by the musical voices of the female tenants as they call to their children playing happily around the dustbins and the artistically arranged washing as it beats against the quaint iron railings, with their colourful coat of rust, is equal to the beauty of anything hanging in the National Gallery.

Indeed, these dwellings are a gallery in themselves and it is up to us, the residents of the borough, to preserve this quaint corner of London. Of course the call of progress must be heeded but surely this piece of London's heritage is worthy of preservation?

H. J. Linglis, Popham Street, N1.

(NB 'Linglis' is obtained from some of the letters of 'Islington')

About the Author

John Rawlings was born in Cornwall Cottages in Islington in 1947 and lived in the same flat with his parents for the next 21 years. He attended Charles Lamb and Highbury County Schools and went on to study architecture. He married Pat, another Islingtonian in 1970. In 1976 their housing situation forced them reluctantly to leave the borough although they still manage to get to the Indian Veg and the Marquess Tavern occasionally. After a relatively short career as a local authority architect he is now retired and lives in Kent with Pat and two grown up daughters. This book grew from notes made twenty years ago about childhood street games. His hobbies are ironing and nostalgia.

Printed in Great Britain
by Amazon